NOWHERE LEFT TO RUN

Life had dealt a bad hand to Bob Steele. A fugitive from the law for a murder he hadn't committed, he was trapped in virtual bondage to Jake Clayborne, a hill-country patriarch who provided protection at a high price. And now that Jake had extended the term of bondage Bob had no choice but to comply, for he knew there was almost no way of escaping from Jake's well-guarded hills.

Then fate added an extra twist in the person of a seventeen-year-old white girl whom Jake had bought from a Cheyenne chief, and Bob was forced to reach a decision. He'd come upon the girl as she hid from Jake in the woods, and the terrible scars on her back convinced him that he couldn't send her back. The only chance the two of them had was to run, but that was really no chance at all—if they got past Jake's guards, Bob was certain to face a hangman's rope for the murder charge against him!

NOWHERE LEFT TO RUN

Todhunter Ballard

GUNSMOKE

This hardback edition 2006
by BBC Audiobooks Ltd
by arrangement with
Golden West Literary Agency

ISBN 10: 1 4056 8105 5
ISBN 13: 978 1 405 68105 6

British Library Cataloguing in Publication Data available.

Printed and bound in Great Britain by
Antony Rowe Ltd., Chippenham, Wiltshire

Chapter 1

Pitchfork Riley eased himself deep to one side of his saddle above the man working at the sluice box beside the little stream, and delivered his laconic message:

"Old Jake says for you to come to the settlement. Today, he says."

Bob Steele quit stirring the mud, lifted out the shovel, put it aside and straightened, looking not at Riley but into the short tunnel in the bank. The digging was going easier today and he did not want to stop.

"What's his all-fired rush? Tomorrow's grocery day."

Riley lifted his shoulders, spat, and thumbed his worn hat well back on his head. "Jake don't do no explaining to me. Maybe he wants you to size up the woman he bought offen the Cheyennes."

Steele turned slowly, his small smile without appreciation. Pitchfork had a macabre sense of humor and Steele nodded. "Sure. Sure."

"It's true, all right." Pitchfork bridled. He had a wide reputation as a liar and when betimes he told a truth he

1

was sensitive about skepticism, and as a clincher he added: "Paid two horses and a gun for her. White woman."

Bob Steele raised an eyebrow. "Now, Pitchfork . . . you trying to tell me Clayborne's got a streak of generosity in him wide enough to pay anything to rescue anybody from anything? I don't believe you."

"No, sir. I didn't say that. It wasn't no rescue. The old devil wanted another woman, and he's keeping her roped up most of the time. Treats her like a slave. It ain't right, and somebody ought to do something about it."

"Who?"

Riley scratched at his scalp and looked piously innocent. "That's a fair question. Somebody could write to Washington, maybe, or the Territorial capital or something. It's agin the law to hold a white woman a slave, ain't it?"

"Go ahead," Steele said without feeling, and went back to shoveling the wheelbarrow load of gravel he had brought out of the little mine into his sluice box.

Riley fidgeted for a while, then rode off in a huff rather than admit that he could not write. Steele watched him out of sight as he headed for the tiny mountain ranch where Jake Clayborne let him run a few head of cattle, a few horses and a clutch of goats.

Bob Steele could not afford to tangle with old Jake Clayborne whatever the provocation. He was a slave here himself. Until tomorrow. He would not even be allowed to leave until then, when he could pay off the last of the bounty money.

Old Jake owned the Medicine Hills, lock, stock, and barrel. Twenty years before he and a crew made up of his three brothers, their sons and grandsons, had arrived, driving a herd of a short thousand Texas cattle that they had pushed

2

across New Mexico and on up into Central Park. The ranchers already filling the big valley had warned him off and he had continued on into the jagged hills and there set up a home ranch in a deep canyon. Dour, resentful, they had built cabins and established the settlement. It had no other name. Then they had sent back to Texas for their families and dug in.

With that core of population Jake had ridden to the Territorial capital and announced to the startled officials that he had three hundred men in the hills. He wanted the Medicines made into a county and if he was refused his whole clan would vote for the damned Democrats. Come to think of it, he'd told them, he'd been raised a Democrat and it wouldn't go against his grain to be one again.

Medicine County was born. Jake Clayborne had himself elected sheriff. Since then, from a combination building that housed the courthouse, the sheriff's office, and the general store, Jake ruled the hills like a king. He permitted a few men outside the family, like Pitchfork Riley, to have small spreads, and there was a slow parade of traffic, people with prices on their heads elsewhere, moving through. They were not there out of the kindness of Jake's heart, but because he wanted every stream, water hole, and grass meadow filed on and fenced. To keep the big ranchers of the Park from running their herds into the hills for summer feed.

The Park people waked up too late, and although they were convinced that the Clayborne clan was not above picking off a few of their animals now and then there was nothing they could do. The feud was a slow-burning standoff.

To that feud Bob Steele owed his liberty, if he could call it that, and possibly his life. In the four years that he had worked in the big valley he had never spoken to a Clayborne until last year. He had risen to be foreman of Don Berry's flourishing small ranch. He was engaged to the daughter of the local banker, and his future looked rosy.

Then Ralph Hume, owner of the huge RH spread, had got grandiose ideas and decided to override Berry's place. There had been raids, running skirmishes, night attacks that Hume blandly blamed on the Claybornes. A showdown came when the Hume riders rounded up all of Berry's young, un-branded stock and threw them into the main corral at the RH headquarters.

Berry had wanted to go to law about it but Bob Steele thought nothing could be proved that way. He chose a time when most of Hume's crew of twenty were scattered over the range, took his six men and went to the RH. With only five Hume riders at the headquarters, and those held off under Steele's guns, they cut the Berry stock out and started them on the drive home. Ralph Hume raged and threatened, and Steele, wanting to avoid a meeting with the bulk of Hume's crew, rode on ahead to scout a clear trail.

During that night someone, Steele still did not know who, hailed Ralph Hume out of his house and shot him dead, and no gun was found near the body.

What happened after that was a nightmare to Steele. First his crew was rounded up and questioned. All of them backed each other, saying none of them had left the cattle until they reached Berry's yard. All of them said that only Steele had gone ahead. They had not seen him again until morning. It was possible that he could have doubled back and murdered Hume. There was no proof either way.

Steele was arrested and charged with murder. Whether his

4

crew had been bought off he could not say. Their testimony was probably true, he thought not one of them would take the initiative to murder a man without his order and he most certainly had not given that. But they were no help to him, and the Hume crew were in town, talking up a lynching. His fiancée visited him at his cell door, not to encourage or help, but to throw his ring in his face and tell him she despised him.

Only Don Berry had believed he was innocent and gone out on a limb for him, wrenched out the cell window with a rope around his pommel and put him aboard a horse with a gun in the boot.

Word of his arrest had spread over the valley like a grass fire under a high wind. The passes, the normal avenues of exit would be closed and watched. In the middle of the night there was only one way out of the hostile Park.

So he had ridden for the Medicine Hills, hoping that the rumors were true, that the sheriff there was sympathetic to a man on the run, that he would be passed on, permitted to make his way to Canada.

He had had a tight time halfway up the first canyon, when a voice hailed him from a dark cabin, told him to turn in and light down, and leave his gun be. He had got off the horse and when he turned he looked into a lamp, shielded at the back. He was looked over, then told to come on inside, and walked into a room that the lamp showed to be rudely furnished, with a door to other quarters in the rear.

The lamp also showed him a man with a shotgun, loosely held but convincing, a tall, thin, hatchet-faced man who asked him in a quiet, nasal voice where he was headed.

Canada, he said.

5

The man nodded, indicated a homemade table and told him to set a spell, hung the lamp on a peg, stoked up a fire in a battered stove and set a coffeepot over the opened lid.

Steele heard soft sound in the back room, a door quietly closing, then a jingle of harness. There wasn't a thing he could do except hope, and right then hope had a very small flame. Without ever turning his back on him the man started a pan of bacon and shoved leftover biscuits into the oven, expertly, with one hand, the other keeping hold of the shotgun. He served the food, joined Steele in a mug of coffee and said not another word. Steele ate and the food lay like a ball in his stomach. He did not care to guess what would happen next.

Within a half hour the harness jingled again, the unseen door opened and closed quietly and his host nodded at the front door. Build yourself a smoke while you can see, he said, then ride on. He waved away Steele's thanks for the food and apology that he had nothing to give in return, lighted the way to Steele's horse, watched him mount and turn back to the trail. Behind Steele the door closed and the lamp went out.

Steele knew that a message had been sent somewhere, that he had been held until the messenger returned. What it meant he could not guess. One thing, he probably would be watched, his progress followed. He rode a mile farther, then hobbled the horse, rolled in the blanket Berry had tied behind the saddle and slept until dawn.

The next day he passed other cabins, set deep in the trees back from the trail, but he was not challenged again. About noon of his second day in the hills he stopped at a stream to drink, to water his horse. As he dipped up water from a shallow pool he stirred the sandy bottom. Bright yellow winked up at him. He sat on his heels and watched the little flake settle heavily again. Then he looked around him.

Upstream from him he saw through the brush a very small, one-room cabin, its door hanging ajar. He walked to it, found it crudely furnished but no blanket on the brown, dried pine boughs on the bunk, no clothing hung on the wall pegs, no sign that anyone was living here. A faint, grass-grown trace led farther up the canyon and at the end of it a mine tunnel, not deep, shoved horizontally into the hillside. There was a small mound of tailings, grass sprouting out of it. There was a weathered sluice box at the edge of the stream.

Obviously the place was abandoned, probably because whoever had opened the mine had found it too unprofitable to put more work into. But there was some gold there. It was a chance, he decided, to pan out some sort of stake before he moved on north of the border.

He had been digging, washing sand for almost a week, recovering three, maybe four dollars' worth of dust a day, and no human being had appeared. He had almost quit wondering about that.

Then he heard a splash, looked up from his shoveling and found three riders unhurriedly crossing the creek. They all carried rifles across their saddles.

Steele's rifle leaned against a tree nearby, ready for game if any should show itself. His revolver was in its belt, but even that was too far away, the direction the other guns were pointing, lazily on him. He straightened carefully, nodded carefully, watched carefully.

It was a fair guess who the old man in the lead was. He had Clayborne written all over him. Steele had seen some of them occasionally in some of the valley stores and they all bore that hatchet-headed, close-eyed stamp. This had to be Jake Clayborne himself. A huge man with thick arms and powerful shoulders. Black shiny eyes set deep in their sockets, a jutting nose like a buzzard's beak. A thin, lipless mouth pulled back to show broken, stained teeth, a smile or a wound.

"Getting rich, boy?" he said in a voice surprisingly high, squeaky as a flustered woman's.

Steele found nothing to say. The big man's mouth widened farther.

"Cat got your tongue?"

"What's there to say?" From Jake Clayborne's reputation he could only expect them to rob him.

The hulking figure shook with a chuckle. "Might say your name. Or you guess that's too risky to say to the Sheriff of Medicine Hills County? Don't need to though. I already seen your picture on a dodger. You're the one shot that Hume rancher. Law down there would like to have you back."

Steele's stomach tightened. His impulse was to deny the charge, but what was the use. No one except Berry in the Park had believed him, and why should this sheriff listen. He stood fair caught and helpless.

Clayborne looked down on him benignly, possessively. "That dodger offers three hundred dollars for the man who brings you in. Three hundred. Tidy sum, ain't it?"

Steele kept his silence, looking directly at the old man, and was startled, puzzled when Clayborne went on.

"You got three hundred dollars' worth of dust yet in your poke?"

Steele shook his head and the old man matched the gesture.

"Nope. You're making maybe three, four a day though. Seems like out of that you could pay me one."

8

"A dollar a day? For what?"

"So's to ease my conscience if I decide not to turn you in and collect that three hundred reward. You would work it off in less than a year and I wouldn't be out of pocket. You'd make a fair stake, then you could ride on."

From despair Steele had a sudden hysterical desire to laugh. Not that the situation was funny, but the old bastard was such an outright thief that he was almost honest about it.

"All right," he'd said. "A dollar a day."

"And you buy your necessaries at the settlement."

That had been two hundred and ninety-nine days ago. Tomorrow the blood money would be paid off and he would be free. Free to leave these hills, but without the stake he had counted on taking with him. Jake's prices at the settlement store had gouged him for an average of another two dollars a day.

In those months he had figured out or seen indications of other tentacles of Jake's profiteering. The little mine was the first trap. There had been others before him who had worked it to pay out rewards offered for them and assure Jake a steady supply of dust. There were other men pocketed through the hills, each doing some chore Jake wanted done, keeping watch, forming a sensitive web of communications to alert Clayborne at its center of any movements throughout his county, a free labor force. A free army, should the Park people take it into their heads to invade the Medicines. He wondered how much of Pitchfork Riley's pitiful handful of animals was destined as tribute to the old pirate.

Just now he wondered what Clayborne wanted now, today, that could not wait until tomorrow and his weekly visit.

There was only one way to find out. He did not like going to the settlement at any time, but there was no choice.

He finished washing out the barrow load of sand, flushed the box with buckets of water from the creek, cleaned the black sand from behind the riffles and panned that down until the iron grains were separated from the tiny flakes of shining gold. These he dried and carried back into the tunnel where no eyes could watch him. He dug up the poke that held his slender horde, added the flakes to it, hid it again in a different spot as he did every day, then dug up the poke in which he kept Jake's ransom and his grocery dust and put them in a pocket.

Then he saddled his horse and turned it toward the settlement.

Chapter 2

<<<<<<<<<<<<<<<<<<<<<<<<<<<<<<<<<<<<<<<<<<<<<<<<<<<<<

The canyon walls rose above him on both sides, heavily timbered, muffling the sounds of the creek in the bottom of the V. The trail climbed away from the creek, a thousand feet above his cabin, seesawed back and forth across the rough face, wound over side draws, and topped out on the mountain crest. There were no trees up here, only solid, bare rock with barely enough soil to support a scant growth of wind-whipped scrub bushes. From this overlook there was a full view of the valley far below where the settlement cabins made an irregular pattern.

Steele left his saddle, moved to the rim and looked down on the combination building in the middle of the big, bare ground, unfenced yard that could be seen clearly over the tops of the descending trees.

With relief he saw no horses tethered at the rail, found no one in sight. That meant that none of Jake's kinsmen, nor any of the outlaws who sought sanctuary under his protection were at the store. Steele had made it his practice from his first day to keep away from the others as much as possible. He did not want to get involved in any of the drunken brawls that often erupted in the settlement.

He was turning back to his horse to ride down when the corner of his eye caught movement below, and he looked back. Jake had come out onto the store gallery, dragging a small, writhing figure after him. Steele saw that it was a woman and that she was struggling against the huge hand that held her, fighting in vain against Jake's enormous strength. The big man back-handed her off her feet, then towed her by her arm across the baked yard.

Bob Steele grunted. He thought that nothing the Claybornes would do could surprise him any longer, but here was brutality beyond need. He was too far away to hear any cries but in the clear telescopic air he watched Clayborne yank her upright and swing her against his whipping post, tie her hands above her head, then bind her ankles to the thick stake, and stalk unhurried back into the store. Steele let out his breath, believing that the show was over, and was turning away again when Jake reappeared, trailing a bullwhip after him.

Steele swore aloud. Even if he were willing to tangle with Clayborne there was nothing he could do. He was too far away. It was an hour's ride down the steep switchbacks of the ragged canyon wall. He stood like a pillar, looking on.

Jake's arm went back, went forward. Steele could not see the whip lash out but the top of the woman's dress split from neck to waist, spread apart, laid her back bare. The next strike tore the skirt and it sagged into a pool of rags around her feet. Naked, she hung, twisting, convulsing as the rawhide curled around her slender body. Jake struck and struck again until there was no longer any reaction to the bite of the whip, until her head lolled back, her long hair fell behind her and the whip tangled and caught in the hair. With a vicious yank he jerked it free, walked to the post, stooped to cut her ankles loose, then rose to slash the thongs that held her arms. The body collapsed. Jake reached for a wrist and with it in one hand and the handle of the whip in the other dragged the woman and the bullwhip, one as limp as the other, back into the store.

If Steele had been in the canyon bottom he thought he might not have been able to hold himself from interfering. The smart thing would be to turn the bay around, go back to the mine, forget.

He was not going to get involved.

He told this to himself aloud, for emphasis. He did not know what had prompted the beating, with Jake's irascibility it could have been any trivial lapse, but in any event there was not a single thing Steele could do for her. It would be impossible to take her out of the valley against the Claybornes without a regiment of soldiers and Steele knew better than to imagine the hard-pressed frontier Army would make any such effort. He told himself all of this. Then he put the horse down the zigzag trail.

The path followed natural ledges, humped over several descending hogbacks, doubled back on itself, doubled again, hidden under the pine and aspens until it broke out on the bench, the foot of the towering peak that brooded over the bowl valley. Still some way ahead was the cluster of buildings that surrounded the headquarters. The hitchrack before the store was still empty.

Steele brought his bay to rest and sat, loose in the saddle, his big body slack and quiet as his gray eyes sought the whipping pole. There was no life in sight. He looked at the clutter of structures. There were no streets as such. The cabins had been set at whatever angles their owners had chosen, each flanked by its small corral or horse shed. Although he could see no one Steele knew that he was watched by many eyes from the dark holes of windows.

He got down from the horse, tethered it and walked past the post without appearing to notice it. There was a red smear at about the level where the woman's wrists had been tied and dark splotches in the gray dust that were also probably her blood. The rags that had been her dress were trailed across the yard where her feet had dropped them. He did not make the mistake of lingering near the post, did not want the watchers to guess that he knew of its recent use. He went on to the store and pushed the scarred door open.

At once Jake Clayborne came through the arch that led to the rear storeroom. He was smiling. A greedy grin that Steele had learned boded trouble. He walked behind his counter, spread his palms on it, wide apart, and leaned forward toward Steele's face, blowing a sour breath to pass for a laugh.

"Glad to see you, boy," he chuckled. "Hated to pull you out of your work, but I didn't want to see you trot in here tomorrow with a last poke full of dust and all primed and packed to ride away from our fair hills, and come on a surprise. Thinking of your best interests, of course."

One hand slapped the counter, then reached underneath to the shelf there, brought up a poster and laid it in front of Steele without letting go of it. Steele looked down on his own face, badly drawn but recognizable, under a black heading.

Under the picture was his name, Robert Steele, in small type as if that were unimportant, and at the bottom in big bold-face again,

ONE THOUSAND DOLLARS.

A chill prescience filled Steele but he said only one word. "Well?"

The raw mouth spread wider. "Ante's gone up, looks like. You're getting to be a real valuable man to some."

Steele's gray eyes went dull, trying to hide anger, and when he said nothing Clayborne went on. He was expansive. Apparently the whipping he had given the woman had put him in a fine humor.

"Seems like young Reggie Hume come on back from school-ing in the East to find out about his daddy's murder and went and raised the reward offer out of his own pocket. Guess he wants you bad. Could be I'd make a friend in the Park if I was to take you down and give you to him. What do you think?"

"You old bastard." The words broke out of Steele before he could stop them, but instead of offending Jake they appeared to be taken as a compliment, and he nodded.

"That's right, that's me, an old bastard that knows what side his bread's buttered on. Now, I can't afford to lose that seven hundred dollars by not turning you in . . . unless . . ." He laid a claw finger alongside his nose, Santa Claus like. "Maybe you'd rather stay around and pay that off your-self?"

"To hell with you." Steele felt that a dam inside him had broken, that he had, at last, to call Jake. "I've taken enough from you. I am pulling out for Canada. And if you try to take me down that hill for that money every outlaw in the

15

Medicines is going to see how little your protection is worth and come down on you hard. Then where is your racket going to be?"

"Well now." Jake's good humor did not fade. "That's a right interesting theory. But Bobby, you're upset and not thinking straight. Give it a little time and you'll know it ain't so. I got a handy passel of kin around here, plenty to take care of anything needs doing. And you go trying to ride out, shucks . . . there's going to be a whole posse put a rope on you right quick. You don't think I'm going to stand hitched and let seven hundred purty dollars just up and leave, do you?"

Bob Steele knew that he was licked. He had known it even as his rebellious words were grinding out, and the knowledge filled him with burning rage. Almost . . . almost, he pulled his gun from the holster and emptied it into Jake's wide chest. But a saving control told him that was a quick way of signing his own death warrant.

He crowded down the impulse, shrugged. Bitterness at the unfair path down which fate was taking him gorged him with burning gall. Where was there justice? Where was there help? It had never been forthcoming when he needed it. Except for Don Berry's rescuing him he had always had to make his own help. Now his old habit took over, face a fact and handle it as best he could.

"All right," he said. "Seven hundred dollars more. As fast as I can pan it. But this time you sign a contract. When I give you that seven hundred that's the end of it."

"Sure." Jake did not hesitate. "Certainly. I respect a man with the gumption to protect his backtracks." He got a stub of pencil from a box on the counter, turned the dodger over and wrote on the back of it.

When Bob Steele pays me a total of one thousand dollars he is a free man to go where he likes.

He signed his name, his thick red tongue twisting between his lips with every stroke of the pencil, then shoved the poster toward Steele.

Steele tore the paper in half, folded the part with the writing on it and stowed it in his pocket. He put no value on it, certain that if he paid out this seven hundred dollars Jake would come up with some other way to milk him. It had only one use. He had watched his fellow fugitives through these months, men who would not honor their own word but would oddly put their faith in the word of another. His gamble was that Jake would believe Steele's agreement, would not watch him too closely. Then Steele would redouble his efforts at the mine, make his dollar a day payments but squirrel away a stake and wait for a chance to slip out of the hills and get away.

Jake, content now with his bargain, whistled a tune, turned to the whiskey barrel on the counter, chose two of the beaten-up cups chained there, none of which had ever been washed, filled them and passed one to Steele.

"Drink up, boy, just to show there's no hard feelings between us."

Neither showed pain as the raw liquor seared their throats. Jake set down his empty cup, wiped at his scruffy mustache and grunted.

"You bring in this week's money? You want groceries today so you don't have to come back tomorrow?"

Steele nodded, not yet able to use his voice, dug out his poke and passed his list across. Clayborne got the meager things together, stuffed them in a sack and weighed out the dust on the scales near the whiskey keg. Steele thought that he would like to have the counterbalance weighed, he was sure it was too heavy to be legal, that he was being further robbed, but again, that was a vain hope.

Finished, Clayborne turned again to the barrel and re-filled the cups. Steele did not want the drink. The first lay like a fireball in his stomach. But he dared not refuse. The stuff came from Jake's own still, was Clayborne's particular pride.

He drank. This time he gagged, barely managed to swallow and Jake hit him on the back, staggering him. Jake's braying laugh filled the cluttered room.

"T'ain't growed up yet, are you, boy."

Steele gasped a thank you for the drink, took the sack and moved quickly out through the door, the laugh following him. He mounted and rode directly out.

The day was late, he would be caught by night before he topped out on the mountain, but he would rather roll in a blanket, hidden up there, than stay any longer in the settlement. Men would be riding in, drinking the rotgut and paying their obeisances and tributes, and he could not stomach that company today.

He was five miles up the grade before he remembered the woman Jake had whipped. Jake's surprise had driven her out of his mind. He was sorry for her, but he was not going to get involved there. She was caught as surely as he in Jake's spider web, in the quicksand of Jake's domination.

Chapter 3

There was a camping spot on the crest, one he had used before, a tumble of mammoth boulders like a crown on the top of the mountain, the mountain's skeleton leached free of soil by eons of weathering. He would rather have gone on to the mine but the trail was too treacherous for night riding. It would be uncomfortable up there, but safer, both from a mishap on the trail and a chance encounter with one of the clan.

He put the horse in among the boulders, tethered it well in behind the rocks, beat the area for snakes and threw his blanket in a gritty, level nest. He did not light a fire, did not want smoke or flame to draw a curious visitor. He did not eat, his stomach still too queasy from Jake's liquor and the shock of his further servitude to tolerate food.

The wind at that altitude was cold and clouds that meant a storm front moving across the range made the night blacker, suffocating. He lay in the lee of a boulder, shivering, trying to sleep, miserable in his mind and his body, stung out of any true rest by flashing, ugly dreams.

With the first faint light, barely enough to show him

shadowy shapes, he gave up, saddled his horse and headed down the west slope, numb to hunger, to thirst. It was noon when he reached the cabin, cared for the horse and turned it into the rough corral, then carried his supply sack inside. He threw a piece of stove wood at a pack rat that crouched beady-eyed on a low rafter, retrieved it and built a fire in the rickety stove, added water to the coffeepot and made a meal of sliced side meat with warmed-over biscuits. He ate without taste, then sat on the log step outside with a second cup of coffee. A lethargy held him. He was unwilling to move, to do anything except sit where he was.

Then he threw the thick dregs, cup and all, onto the ground, got up and walked along the creek to the tunnel entrance, forcing his mind to concentrate on working. Only work could save him. The more gold he could wash out of the stubborn gravel the sooner he could make his try to escape. He held that as a lodestone to keep himself functioning.

He was halfway through the second barrel when he sensed another presence, turned with dull resentment, expecting to find that old Jake had sent one of his many grandnephews to make sure he had not bolted, that he was indeed digging out more gold for the patriarch. Then he straightened, so abruptly that a muscle in his back spasmed against the sudden demand on it.

It was not a Clayborne boy, but a woman, watching from the edge of the brush, poised there like a doe ready for flight yet held by some force he could not name.

The only woman he had spoken to in this last year was Pitchfork Riley's slovenly, three-hundred-pound wife. The only women he had seen were Clayborne women, at a distance, and he had been careful not to try to talk to any of them. He might, he thought, be looking at a ghost.

Or a witch. Long yellow hair was a tangled mass around her head and shoulders. The dress hanging from her bony frame was a flour sack. The face was gaunt, making the eyes look larger to remind him again of a doe, a doe's terror darkening them. Her legs were bare, her feet ludicrous in a boy's worn-out boots. His first impression was of a wizened crone, then he saw that her face was young, if sunken.

He stood awkwardly, openly gawking, and after a long moment during which they were both very still she apparently decided that he was not going to chase her. In a swift run with her hands stretched in pleading before her she crossed the twenty feet between them, her lips moving. Not until she stopped almost against him could he hear her words, repeated over and over in an urgent whisper.

"Help. Please help. Please help me . . ."

Bob Steele jumped back, holding the shovel handle as a fence between them, but his words were jerked from him by instinct.

"What's happened to you?"

"Everything . . . I have to get away . . . From Jake Clayborne . . . Escape . . ."

It seemed to Bob Steele that his heart plummeted into his stomach as a lead weight. The boughten woman of Pitchfork Riley's story. The writhing figure he had seen tied to a post and whipped unconscious with a bullwhip. He had been too far away to see what she looked like then. Now she was here. Too close. On his doorstep. And she was trouble. Steele took a long, uneven breath. His voice came gruff. It stuck in his throat.

"Nothing I can do. Clear out of here."

She took another step forward, leaning toward him, insistent, as though she had not heard him or thought he had not heard her.

"Help. They'll come after me."

"Indeed they will. How did you get loose anyway?"

She hurried her words then, pointing behind her. "Sneaked out . . . Jake was drunk . . . I got a horse from the corral and . . ."

He snapped at her. "Where is it now?"

She shook her head, reaching pathetically for hope in his question, her voice an unemotional monotone, rushing to get the questions out of the way before time ran out.

"It threw me . . . back aways . . . I didn't have a saddle, didn't dare try to get one . . . Please. Hurry."

Hurry at what? Steele's mouth tightened in a bitter line. What did she expect him to do? Why should he be expected to do anything? She was none of his affair. This country was hard on women, wife-beating was not uncommon, was generally shrugged at, and since his banker's daughter fiancée had taken the word of a hysterical town against his, had so easily broken faith with him, he had little sympathy with any of her sex. He was in no position to help anyone, man or woman, break Jake's stranglehold on them. Though he was planning to try to make a run for Canada himself his rational mind told him it was impossible. Jake simply had too many men, with every trail into or out of the Medicines watched by someone Jake had posted there, all of them indebted in one way or another. Every one of them would stop anyone who tried to pass, to secure their own positions and because if they did not they would bring Jake's violent wrath down on their own heads.

Steele blew out an angry snort. "Don't look to me. I'm just as much a captive as you are."

The dark eyes widened farther, bewildered, curious. "I don't understand. How can he hold you? Can't you just ride out?"

"No. No more than you can. And what I ought to do is put you on a horse and take you back to the settlement as fast as I can. It might make me some points with Jake and it would be a lot easier on you."

"But you won't do that." She said it quickly, confident.

"What makes you so sure?"

She looked at him directly, as if she read something in his face. "You wouldn't. I just know."

He was too long in deciding, then he laughed sourly. "Then you know more than I know. I will do this. There's a gentle little buckskin in the corral, an extra horse. I won't give you a saddle because it can be traced back to me, but nobody except Pitchfork Riley knows about the buckskin. Take it and go any direction you choose. You won't get far on any trail. Your only chance is to ride back to the settlement voluntarily. Maybe Jake won't be as hard on you as if he has to catch you. At least you'll be safe and fed there. The Claybornes take care of their own."

"Safe?" The voice broke in a low, strangled scream. She spun around, bent and flung the hem of the flour sack up above her shoulders.

The fair skin of her back was brutalized by the raw welts of the bullwhip. Although he had watched the beating he was not prepared for the close view of the cruel cuts. She should not have been able to stand up for a week, let alone ride a horse bareback over the mountain.

"God Almighty . . ." The words wrenched out. He did not know he spoke aloud. He would have looked away but could not. Beneath the fresh lashes was a crosshatch of older scars, healed but not faded. She could not have been in the settlement that long without his hearing of her. "Who whipped you before?"

She dropped the sack dress back, her voice coming through it muffled. "Cheyennes. They killed my mother and father and the rest of the wagon train, but Red Cloud kept me for his woman."

"And beat you?"

"His squaws did . . . They didn't want me in the lodge and Indian women appear to have ways of making the men's lives hell when they want to. That's why Red Cloud was glad to sell me to Clayborne . . . for two horses and a rifle. He saved face. That's a good price for any woman." She was turning, letting him see the bitterness in her down-turned mouth. "And I thought I was being rescued . . . this big, bearded, noble man was saving me from the Indians. I was better off with Red Cloud. No Indian could hold a candle to Jake Clayborne for sheer meanness."

On that point Bob Steele could heartily agree, and in agreeing he felt a curious lessening of his animosity for her. And when she went on, looking up at him in bold puzzlement, saying, "But you . . . what makes you so afraid of the Claybornes?" he began to talk.

He had not talked about the troubles before to anyone. The bush telegraph the clan maintained had already spread the story through the hills by the time he found the mine. Even Pitchfork Riley had heard a garbled version and he had known instinctively that it would be useless to deny his guilt. In his encounters at the settlement he had found that his fellow refugees considered it cowardly, insulting to them, of anyone trying to plead innocence. He felt more relief than he would have believed in telling this woman why he was here, why he could not leave, watching her listen and accept his words as truth.

"But if you didn't kill that rancher, why did you run?" she had prodded him.

He thought back to the hearing in the judge's chambers, to the ominous, angry crowd that gathered so quickly in the street outside the courthouse, and the white, scared faces of the two deputies set to guard the office. He had trusted the town, the people he had known well and liked through his four years in the valley. He had believed that they liked him, that he would be given a fair hearing at the trial, and he had intended to stand for that trial. Until, locked in the cell, he had seen one deputy and then the other go off shift and leave the jail, and later seen the sheriff himself quietly go out and leave the jail door ajar. He had known then, incredibly, that nothing except the open bars of the cell front and an easily broken padlock on the door were between him and certain lynching.

"I've never killed anyone in my life," he told her, "but if I had not run I'd have been a dead man before that night was over."

"I don't understand why," she said. "If you had a good reputation why would they all turn against you like that?"

He gave her a twisted smile. "It took me awhile to puzzle that out myself. But it figured. The big ranchers wanted to keep the little fellows in line, keep them from growing into a challenge of their power. The man I rode for was small, not important. What was important to the big men was that someone had dared to kill Ralph Hume, from ambush. If it could happen to Hume it could happen to anybody. So somebody had to hang for that murder and I was the handiest. I'd had the audacity to go after the stock

Hume had appropriated from Berry. It had to be shown that the little man did not argue with the big man. As for a trial . . . There was no evidence against me and it was possible I'd be acquitted. They couldn't take that chance. They had to prove their point."

She shook her head, saying, "It's hard to accept that idea. They sound a lot like Jake Clayborne himself."

"They are," he agreed, "although both the Central Park ranchers and Jake would deny it. But I am trapped between them with no way to fight back. Why try to fight when you haven't anything to fight with?"

"You've quit." She said it in a kind of wonder as if the idea of anyone stopping a struggle against forces that oppressed him was beyond her comprehension.

For his part, he was convinced of her foolishness in thinking she could win over Jake Clayborne.

"How old are you?" he said suddenly.

"Nearly eighteen."

"How long were you with the Indians?"

"About three weeks."

"And with Clayborne?"

"One week today."

He started to say that after she had been with Jake a year, after she had endured his whippings, she would learn to give up too. He did not. Somehow he knew that at this point he could not make her see the uselessness of resisting. A heavy weariness overcame him, a pity for her, and in spite of his knowledge that he could do nothing to help even if he wanted to, a sense of guilt chilled him. He shook it off with a vicious shrug and pointed insistently up the trail.

"You'd better believe me. The only smart thing for you

to do is take the buckskin and ride back to the settlement on your own, before they find you."

"No. Never. I am not going back there alive."

"All right." Futility make his voice a harsh sigh. "Come on, then, I'll get the horse for you."

"Wait, please." She spoke hurriedly. "Could I take some food with me? I haven't eaten since yesterday."

He almost swore. Her face was so gaunt, her eyes so big, but the pressure of time was on him. He wanted her as far away from him as she could get before Jake caught up with her. He spun toward the cabin, in a hurry now to get her food, put her on the horse and get her out of there. He did not follow the path that wound along the creek. It was quicker to cut through the brush over the little hogback and he charged up the slope. In his anxiety he gave no thought to snakes, although it was the season when the reptiles were changing their skins, were restless, dangerous.

He heard the buzz. Instinctively he jumped aside. His boot heel caught on a rock, twisted his ankle and dropped him to the ground. The striking snake buried its fangs in the back of his leg above the top of his boot, sinking its venom deep.

He thrashed to his feet and for an instant the heavy body hung, its mouth caught in the trousers cloth, writhing in ugly convolutions. He shook his leg in panic, shook the snake loose and as it fell, trying to coil again, he tramped it into the hard ground, his heavy boot soles stomping the life out of the flailing muscle. He did not dare stop until his heel caught the flat head squarely and he ground it into bloody shapelessness.

Rage held him in a frenzy, rage not at the snake but at

his own carelessness, an inexcusable mistake. Never before had he crossed this ground without a pole in hand to beat the brush ahead of him. The small ridge was alive with these creatures and he seldom traveled the path along the stream without killing at least one of them. Now he had let his anxiety over getting the girl away make him forget the more present danger. And he would pay heavily for it.

He stared down at the body that still twitched and slithered from side to side. The pit of his stomach contracted. He had seen victims of snake bite. He knew what would happen as the venom spread through his body, paralyzed one nerve after another. Within fifteen minutes he would break out in a cold sweat, would be unstable on his feet. Then he would begin to vomit as the enervating prostration set in. His pulse would rise, then plummet, his eyes would go out of focus, dilate until vision was uncertain. And death would probably follow within twelve hours.

Whatever chance he had of doing anything to save himself would have to be done quickly, while he was still master of his senses and in control of his reflexes. He waved the girl after him and hobbled down to the cabin, stopping outside where there was light. He flung off his gunbelt, pulled out the belt that held his trousers, used it to wrap a tourniquet around his leg and ripped the trousers leg wide.

White faced, the girl watched, her eyes enormous, then she caught the idea, picked up a stick, thrust it under the belt and twisted, tightening until all the blood flow was shut off from the lower part of the leg.

Steele looked down, helpless from here on. The position of the wound made it impossible for him to reach the two livid spots with his mouth. But the girl was already working, anchoring the stick, reaching for the heavy bladed knife in the sheath at his waist, saying in a flat voice:

"This will hurt. Can you stand still?"

He nodded, and felt the blade drive into his leg with a burning stroke and thought that she must have cut clear to the bone. He cried out involuntarily but she did not stop. He felt the blood flowing, then felt the drawing as she put her mouth to the slash and sucked deeply. She drew back, spat out the blood and sucked again and emptied her mouth. Her face was even whiter now and she gagged.

At that sound he turned quickly away and began to vomit. Retching in spasms it seemed to him that it would never stop, that it would tear the lining from his stomach, then it ended in a series of dry heaves and he clung to the side of the door for support, expecting to collapse at any moment.

He kept his feet, then suddenly his whole body was chilled with cold sweat and he shivered although the sun was hot. His head began to swirl. His eyes lost focus, the pupils dilated. He ached to let his knees fold, to drop to the ground and drift into unconsciousness, but he fought against it. If he left the tourniquet tight too long he would invite gangrene. He muttered thickly:

"Loosen it. The belt."

His foot and lower leg were numb. When she released the band blood rushed down like fire, filled his foot with burning needles. He bit his lips on the pain and when it eased told her:

"Now tighten it again. Then take the buckskin and get out of here while you can. It's only a matter of time until Jake tracks you."

She looked up from where she knelt, shaking her head. "Who would take care of you?"

Surprise shocked him into concentrating. Incredibly she was willing to stay, to look after someone she did not know, to risk being captured by Clayborne. It went against all reason. He leaned against the doorjamb, swaying there.

"No. You've done all you can. Nobody else would have done as much. If I'm going to die I'll do it within the next twelve hours. If I'm still alive tomorrow morning I'll probably make it. But if Jake comes here and finds you it won't matter whether I lick the poison. He'll kill me out of hand and probably you too."

She came up to her feet, her breath drawing in noisily. That alternative had not apparently occurred to her. And in that moment they heard horses on the canyon trail.

Jake.

The name flashed in his mind, in her eyes. Steele shook his swirling head trying to clear it.

"Go." His words were thick, hard to understand. "Around the cabin . . . up along the ridge . . . Quarter mile above my mine . . . another hole . . . someone followed a vein . . . only twenty feet long but the entrance is overgrown. I don't think anyone else knows it's there. Stay in there until I come . . . tell you it's safe . . ."

He pushed away from the jamb, fell, fumbled for the gunbelt and held the big Colt up to her.

"They find you . . . shoot Jake . . . many as you can . . . but keep one bullet for you . . ."

She did not argue any longer. She took the gun and was gone. He lay for a moment listening to the approaching horses. They seemed not to concern him now, not to matter. Dizzy, totally tired, he got his knees under him and crawled into the single dim room and hauled himself up onto the narrow bunk.

Chapter 4

The solid bunk, nailed against the cabin wall, swayed like a hammock in a high wind. The room slowly revolved. Steele lay gasping, his knuckles white as he clung to the bunk side and fought the sleep that wanted to envelop him. He talked to himself aloud, about the leg, telling himself that he must stay conscious, that he must soon ease the tourniquet again, let the blood course down into the veins in his foot.

Awkward, with much effort, he finally managed to sit up, reach down to the belt. The girl had tucked the stick under its edge. He worked clumsily. The leg was swelling, discolored now, streaked with purple and red, feeling twice its normal size. He groaned. He had to keep the blood flowing through that swollen member or it would pustulate, turn gangrenous. If that happened he was doomed even though he beat the venom. He might live for weeks, but the poison would finally destroy him. He felt the stick dig into the swollen flesh with new sharp pain, and forced it out, felt relief as the leather gave, and then the fire again in his foot. He dropped back on the tumbled blanket, all of his strength given to keeping awake. His head burned, his skin was dry and his lips were cracking. His senses were wandering.

Jake Clayborne was standing in the cabin door. Jake was there. Jake . . . or a dream?

Jake. Steele did not know how long he had been there. And he was not alone. Three men squeezed through the entry after him, crossed the room to stand above the bunk. Through his blurred vision he could not be sure who they were, except that one was Jake's nephew, Job. He knew that by the high, nervous laughter.

He tried to gather his wits, to tell why they were there. There was a reason, there must be, but it was like trying to think through dense fog. He could not capture the sense of it. The leg was not hurting then, was beyond the grasp of his mind.

His shoulders were seized. He was hauled up, sitting. His eyes found Jake's face within inches of his own. Jake was shaking him, shouting.

"Answer me . . . Where is she? Tell me before I choke you dead."

The movement shot pain through him again that stabbed through his consciousness, brought back the girl's image like a puzzle falling into place. His tongue went around his lips and it was not hard to dissemble.

"Snake," he said weakly. "Snake bit me . . ."

Jake quit shaking him, shoved him back on the pillow, looked down his frame. "What the hell?" he said, sounding puzzled.

Steele rocked himself up again, felt for the belt and again tightened it, gouging himself with the stick but making it secure. Jake peered down at the swollen leg as if he thought it was some kind of trick.

"Where'd you get that?" he said suspiciously.

Steele gagged with pain and weakness. "Up at the mine. Cut through some brush . . . like damn fool . . ."

Job Clayborne giggled again, came forward to his uncle's side. He was as tall as Old Jake but scrawnier. Steele felt rather than saw that he watched the leg with a sadistic satisfaction and the voice held a pleased awe.

"You ain't going to make it, man. You plumb ain't."

Jake shoved him off with a rough paw. "Get out of here."

Job retreated a step but did not take his eyes off the leg. "He's gonna die. You wanta bet he don't?"

"He'll die." Jake's high, womanish voice climbed with the intensity of his anger. "He'll die sure unless he tells me right now where Bella's hiding."

So her name was Bella. This was the first time he had thought about a name for her. It had not seemed to matter. His head rolled in a slow negative.

"I don't know what you're talking about."

Jake grabbed him roughly again, shouting. "Don't you lie to me. We found her horse less than half a mile from here and her boot tracks led straight this way."

Warning bells clanged through Steele's grogginess. He knew he dared not risk saying anything more, his brain was not functioning well enough to play games with Clayborne. He simply looked at the man and his silence infuriated Jake more than another denial would have done. The huge hand let go its hold on his shoulder and the fist smashed into Steele's face.

The blow knocked him back on the bed and Jake lifted his thick boot, slammed it against the swollen leg.

Steele shrieked, unable to stop the sound, but he was

rewarded when a wave of sheltering blackness smothered him in merciful unconsciousness.

He came awake gasping as a bucket of cold water was doused over his face. He sputtered, trying to clear his mouth and nose and opened his eyes. Job was there again, grinning at him, nodding sagely.

"Looks like he done come to, finally."

Once more Jake elbowed his nephew aside and spoke in what was for him a reasonable voice.

"I don't like to hurt you, Bob. You and me have played fair with each other, ain't we? But I won't stand for no bastard . . . no bastard at all making free with my woman."

Steele used a corner of the blanket to mop water out of his eyes. The dousing had cleared his mind somewhat and he said in an exhausted voice:

"I suppose it won't do any good to tell you I just don't know what you're talking about."

"It ain't you I'm blaming." Jake turned wheedling. "I know you never had a chance to see her or talk to her before today. But she come here, over the mountain. We followed her path clear as chicken droppings. We found where the horse threw her. She lit in the brush and like to broke it down, then she come stumbling down this way. She got in the stream and we lost her, but there ain't no place else she could have gone."

"If she came to the cabin I wasn't here to see her. I was up at the mine. Getting snake bit."

He could not tell whether Jake believed him, but Job cut in, his eyes narrowed.

"If that's a real bite why didn't you come to us for help?"

Steele lied. "I would have, but I couldn't make it. Couldn't have got a saddle on a horse . . . couldn't have got up."

Job's eyes glittered like polished glass, suspicious, speculative, and even in his numbed condition Steele knew suddenly that Job was more dangerous than old Jake had ever been, with an animal shrewdness that he feared could penetrate his mind. To escape he let himself sink again, drift off toward a welcome coma. He was jerked out of it viciously.

"Don't go to sleep on me." Jake hit him again, breathing nosily through his open mouth. "I want that woman. I want her now." Another blow crashed against his cheek, split the skin above his high cheekbone.

Job's studied voice said, "Hit him like that again and you'll kill him."

"I'll kill him. That's what I aim to do."

"Before he tells you where she is?"

Jake's breathing rasped louder and over it Job said:

"I'm starting to think he's telling the truth. A dying man don't lie often and from the look of that leg I'd say he's about had it for sure. What's he got to gain? You kill him, he'll die a lot easier than from snake bite. I don't think he ever heard of her. I was watching his eyes when you said her name."

"But that horse, and the boots leading this way?"

"She took to the stream, likely she waded past here while he was in the mine like he said. She could have taken off through the hills. Let's go out and look around a bit. Steele ain't going no place soon and that's for certain." As he talked his sharp eyes surveyed the room. He saw the rifle on its hooks against the wall and took it down. "Where's your short gun?"

Without hesitation Steele said, "Should be in my belt outside the door. If it isn't, then I dropped it when I fell trying to get away from the snake . . . or along the trail while I was trying to make the cabin."

Job went outside and came back with the empty belt. There was blood drying on it. He showed it to Jake.

"I'd say he shucked it to doctor that leg. But the gun wasn't there. Let's look up the trail, in the mine, while there's still some light."

They trooped out and now at last Steele sank into deep sleep. They did not come back to disturb him. He woke once during the night to total silence, then slept again. He woke a second time and lay wide-eyed, listening. Some sound had roused him. At first he thought it was the pack rat, but it came again and he knew it was a footstep on the cabin floor and a nightmare terror gripped him. He lay rigid, unable to move, to protect himself. Then he heard her voice, a low whisper.

"Mister . . . Mister . . ."

As he did not know her full name, she apparently did not know his. Relief flooded him, but his answering whisper grated with urgency.

"Get away from here. They may still be around."

"They rode off. I watched them go." She had groped to the bedside, fumbled and her hand found his forehead. "It's more than twelve hours. Are you all right?"

For an instant he did not know what twelve hours meant, then it registered. His foot and shin as far as the knee were without feeling, but he was alive. He had a chance now. It was still slim, but it was there. He wanted to shout it. He had not realized until then how great was his revulsion at the face of death. He clamped his mouth closed on the sound. The girl said that the Claybornes had ridden away . . . but had they really? He remembered the lingering suspicion in Jake's hard eyes. They could have pretended to leave, laid a trap into which she had walked. Anger that she had disobeyed his order came through his voice.

"I told you to stay hidden until I came. You shouldn't have come back here."

"I'm starving . . . and they're gone," she insisted.

Dully he knew that it was true she needed food. Her withered little frame could not have energy enough stored in it to sustain her much longer without eating, and he said grudgingly:

"There's jerky and cold biscuits in the cupboard."

He heard her fumble across the room and bump into the single table in the kitchen area. Then in horror he heard a match struck, saw the tiny flame silhouette her as she lifted the smoked chimney of the lamp on the table and lit the oil-soaked wick. The light came up as she replaced the chimney.

"For God sake, kill that lamp." But his hoarse whisper was too late. The glow was a fact, undeniable. A message sent to anyone who might be watching outside. "No," he countermanded his order. "Leave it. Grab some food and get out. Go through the wood hole beside the stove."

She moved quickly but it seemed to him agonizingly slow, rummaging through the box he had nailed against the wall for a cupboard. She straightened with a piece of jerky in one hand, three biscuits in the other. It was then they heard the sound. The jingle of harness as a horse on the trail shook its head. She turned and was gone, so quickly and quietly that in his fuzziness he almost believed she had not been there.

He threw back the blanket and swung his feet to the floor and judged the distance from the bed to the table. He had to cross that distance. He had to prove to whoever was coming that he could leave the bunk and light the lamp.

The room was chill with the canyon draft that whipped through the open door. The shirt he had slept in was soaked with sweat, clammy with it, and the combination of fever and cold sent shivers racking up and down his body. He tried to gather himself, wondering if this was how death came, crowding upon you, weighing you down with a greater load than you could bear.

He heard the wind, bringing the noise of horses, and with that to give him a spurt of strength he labored up, lurched toward the table and reached it falling, twisting, sinking onto the chair beside it. He was sitting there with his arms folded on the table top, his head resting on them when Jake Clayborne filled the doorway. With effort Steele lifted the great burden of his head. He saw Clayborne stopped inside the door, staring his surprise at finding the snake-bitten man out of bed, heard the disbelief in his question.

"How did you get there?"

"Walked." The tone was exhausted.

"Why the light?"

"Didn't want to die . . . in the dark."

They watched each other, Jake's suspicion a raw force in the room. He went around the table and peered into the dim lean-to kitchen. Steele made a quiet prayer that the girl had pushed the trap door shut. He had built it to save himself the trouble of carrying stove wood around and through the main room. Clayborne turned back, puzzled but not convinced, saying:

"I didn't figure you had the strength to move off that bunk. Seemed to me Bella lit that lamp, that she sneaked in after we left. We made enough noise getting out, wanted her to think we were gone for good.

"Stand up."

The order startled Steele. "What?"

"Stand up. I want to see how you can walk on that leg."

Steele dragged himself erect, took the three steps to the bunk and dropped on the tumbled blanket. Jake growled his admission that it could be done, but said doggedly:

"I still think you're lying and if I find out so I'll skin you and stretch your hide on the corral fence."

Steele did not try to answer that. He watched the big man back out through the door then heard him grunt as he mounted and put his horse up the trail. He looked at the lamp on the table. He was short of oil. He hated to leave it burning but the effort of reaching it again was too much.

"To hell with it," he mumbled. He was tired. Too tired. He had used up his strength. The strength needed to survive. And what did a dead man need with coal oil?

He closed his eyes. This time there was less of the wheeling dizziness spinning in his head. He opened his eyes, turned them to the lamp. The double vision was gone. Maybe, just maybe, he was going to live. He dropped his eyelids again, and this time drifted off into a heavy, dreamless sleep.

Chapter 5

<<<<<<<<<<<<<<<<<<<<<<<<<<<<<<<<<<<<<<<<<<<<<<<

He waked cold. He had not wrapped the wet blankets around him and Clayborne had left the door wide open. The lamp was out, its oil bowl dry and there was the stink of charred wick in the air. He moved, heavily limp in all his muscles except the leg. That was stiff and without feeling. His lips were cracked from his fever but that interior burning had broken.

He was alive.

Thirst gnawed at him, the dehydration of long sweating parched his throat. He rolled carefully off the bunk and crawled to the water bucket and drank. The water chilled him further. Dragging a blanket with him he crawled across the packed earth floor, through the open door and lay, resting from the effort in the grass of the sunlit yard. The position of the sun made it nearly noon. His stomach was empty and as warmth seeped into him he became aware of hunger, but it was not compelling enough to force him into the further exertion of trying to reach the kitchen.

He was encouraged. He had heard that a victim of snake bite, once past the crisis hours, made a miraculous recovery.

His head was now clear, his vision sharp and his pulse had stopped oscillating. There was only the leg now to give him trouble. It was still numb. He wrestled with himself to sit up, to twist to investigate it.

It was swollen, the skin stretched tight. It was blotched with discoloration. And now thin red lines ran down the calf to hypnotize him. Blood poisoning was setting in.

His fingers found the gashes the girl had cut to drain the bite. They had scabbed over and he suspected there was pus gathered underneath. Now he had to move. He got on his feet, hobbled in to the stove and built a fire, put the water bucket over the open lid and shoved the coffeepot against it, then he pulled a chair close to the stove and sat down to wait.

The coffee was ready first, two days old, black and bitter, but its warmth helped. He finished a cupful before the bucket began to steam. And then the girl came again, slipping through the wood box panel, almost colliding with his chair.

He jumped as if she were another snake, so sudden was her appearance, so unexpected, and a rage with her filled him like adrenelin, made him want to shout at her. He clamped his teeth against the sound and spoke through them, viciously.

"What the hell are you trying to do, deliberately get us both killed? To come down here in broad daylight . . . don't you understand that Jake's got eyes in the back of his head? You can bet on it he's got somebody watching this place."

She stood up, brushing dirt from her hands, shaking her head, her eyes level, her voice confident and vaguely accusing.

"No he has not. You worry too much. I made very certain.

There is no one in the brush. There are no horses anywhere near." She gave his face a critical survey and said in a flat statement, "You're better. Let me see your leg."

He did not know why she asked, she did not wait for permission but bent and studied the scabs, the thin red lines. "Those will have to be opened and cleaned out good."

He glowered at her and waved a hand at the steaming bucket. "I know. I was about to . . ."

She did not wait for him to finish, went to the wall and took his towel from the peg, dipped one end in the hot water and folded it against the dry section. Then she clapped the smoking cloth against the wound. He wrenched away, gasping, snapping at her.

"Too hot. You'll scald me."

"It has to be." She said it without sympathy, without emotion. "To draw the blood . . . and the poison." She caught and held the leg and forced the cloth against it again.

He shuddered but grudgingly he knew that she was right. He sat enduring as she dipped the towel again and again, cooling it only to where she herself could barely touch it. The scabs loosened, softened. She sponged them off, sponged out the pus pockets under them. The area around the wound was the color of a boiled lobster as the heat brought the blood rushing to it. And gradually it brought the red lines shrinking toward the cuts too. His shirt, his face were soaked again with sweat started by pain before she finished and stood back.

"We'll leave it open awhile now," she announced. Then she got his washbasin from the bench, dipped hot water into it, cooled it slightly and scrubbed her hands, emptied the pan and refilled it and set it on the table. "Wash yourself off while I get us something to eat," she said. "You'll feel better."

Still angry, but helpless to do anything about her, he humped his chair to the table obediently. The water did freshen him, relax him somewhat, then he sat watching her at the stove. Unwillingly he conceded that she had been through a lot recently, particularly these last few days, yet here she was, ragged, unkempt, hunted, pragmatically making pan biscuits, frying salt meat, heating a pan of beans he had cooked the day before he had gone to the settlement, making fresh coffee. She took away the pan of water, served him a plate and put it with a cup before him, served herself and sat down opposite him. If she ate more ravenously than good manners dictated he understood the reason and forgave her that. But they ate in a brittle silence.

He finished first and waited until she was finally filled, then he said, "Now you're fed, and you've got me on the mend. Thank you for that. But take something with you and clear out of here."

One corner of her mouth turned up, not in a smile. "And leave you with the dirty dishes? Two sets of them? When you're not in shape to stand up and do them?"

She left the table and began cleaning the kitchen of proof that Steele was not alone. He could only groan, watching her like a hawk until she had put away the last evidence, then he said sharply:

"Now . . . now. Will you take the buckskin and get the hell away?"

She was deliberately slow in turning to face him, and her eyes held a dark anger of their own.

"You are a very difficult man, aren't you. Like a grizzly with a hurt paw. No. I will not leave you until I know the

43

blood poisoning is licked and that that leg is not going to kill you. You got that snake bite while you were trying to help me, much as you didn't want to. I pay my debts. Mr. Man, I will go back to my little tunnel and hide. You soak out that leg again tonight and I'll be down in the morning."

His complete helplessness to control her turned his anger to pleading. He held both hands toward her, the palms up.

"Please . . . Please . . . use a little sense. If you won't leave, at least don't come here in daylight any more."

"All right. You probably know Jake better than I do, so I'll come tomorrow night." Then she ducked out through the trap door and was gone.

He humped the chair across to the bunk and rolled into that and slept, weak and exhausted. In late afternoon he roused and checked his wound, found it scabbing again and the red streaks still angry. He soaked the crusting away, cleaned the cuts, this time tore up a clean towel and wrapped it around the leg. He drank some coffee, sat in the chair, but by dark he was in the bunk and he slept completely through the night.

The next morning he felt better, a little stronger. The swelling in the leg was going down and the frightening red lines seemed paler. He soaked and rebandaged, ate a little and spent the day lying outside, resting and watching the hillsides. He saw no one. He could not hope that the Claybornes had given up. They were probably combing the far side of the mountain.

The girl came just after dusk, as quietly as before. He had cooked up a fresh pot of beans and added to the coffee. She treated the leg again and in the near darkness it appeared improved. They ate by the light from the stove. The lamp was not refilled and he did not want to use it anyway, with her in the cabin. Then without his telling her she slipped away. In the empty gloom he was surprised at a curious loneliness.

That was a new experience for him. He had been increasingly a loner ever since he had run away from the Ohio farm when he was thirteen, too often finding people he could not trust. The four good years in the Park had tempted him out of himself. Then had come the debacle there to shatter emerging faith.

He had slept so much since the bite that he was now too awake for bed. He rolled a cigarette, limped in to light it from a sliver shoved in between the draft bars of the stove, then hobbled out to the dark yard. An owl high on the ridge hooted in its isolation. The stars were cold, far away, with no companionship about them tonight. A mountain cat cried into the dark and for a few moments the other wild sounds stopped, then as if reassured that the hunting animal was not stalking them, one and then another of the small nocturnal scurryings began again.

Steele felt a sudden kinship with those creatures that lived out wary lives as prey. Here he sat, tuned for the sound of Clayborne horses, his breathing shallow with the waiting for it. He knew they were still searching. The girl had to be somewhere in the hills. She could not have gotten out without being seen by someone. They would bide their time, waiting for some signal along the lines of the web.

If only his strength would come back. But what then? How could they deceive themselves that they could get away? And if they should, where would they go? Unaware that it had happened he was thinking in terms of *they*, not *each*. Alone, each would have a choice, granted the miracle of getting through the hills. Together there was none.

Northward lay the Indian reservation and the Indian police made certain that no white man without authorization crossed the tribal lands, and surely that would be the last place the girl would want to go. If she were caught, Red Cloud would deem himself duty bound to return her to the man he had sold her to.

South spread the big Park where the sheriff waited for Steele, made more eager to take him by the added reward offered by Reggie Hume.

Steele knew Reggie, had seen him at roundups, at dances in the schoolhouse, in the saloons of Maxwell. He had not liked the arrogant, spoiled boy, accustomed to wealth, to giving orders, to having his own way. Neither did Reggie waste love on Steele, because Linda Thorne had chosen a mere foreman to promise herself to and had not even a smile for the heir to the Hume ranch. That Linda had broken her promise would not placate Reggie. If Steele were to be seen in the Park, Reggie would have the whole huge crew the big ranch supported out to hunt him down.

On the west rose the main spine of the Rockies. High peaks separated by deep, impassible canyons through which there were no trails.

The east was cut off by a long arm of the Park, as dangerous to be found in as the main valley.

They could neither fly through the sky nor burrow under the ground. They had no options at all.

At first the girl had meant nothing, a faceless stranger caught in the mesh of circumstances, unfortunate but not his responsibility. She was still a stranger, he did not even know her last name. Yet she had saved his life, and that was more than anybody except Don Berry had ever done for him before. Tonight the picture of her in Jake Clayborne's hands again tied his stomach in a tight, sick knot. The thin, starved figure. The back whipped raw . . . She had risked herself to help with his leg and until this minute he had not even thought that he might have done something about that back.

He cursed himself, pushed angrily to his feet and fumbled into the cabin, threw himself on the bunk. Churning thoughts kept sleep at bay. Then another specter rose to mock him. Two people ate more than one. If they both stayed here his next grocery list would betray them to Jake, beyond doubt.

He had still not found any chink in the impasse when she came down from the tunnel the next evening, but now he could not bring himself to tell her the new danger. His leg was definitely better, the swelling all but gone, the red poison gone, although soreness kept him limping heavily.

As they ate he almost suggested that she stay in the cabin that night, where it was warmer, that he would go to the tunnel. There had been no sign of Claybornes for over three days now and he had begun to hope that they would not come this way again. But he did not. He could not predict old Jake.

The next morning he dragged his small tin tub into the sunny yard, filled it with two pails of warm water and had his first bath in nearly a week while he soaked the leg once more. He dressed in fresh clothes, then limped to the pole corral to feed the horses that had taken short shrift through these days.

From there he saw the riders at the far reaches of the little meadow. They had not come down the canyon but from the west, and for a moment he did not recognize them. He watched, uneasy, uncomfortable at being unarmed. The Claybornes had carried off his rifle and the girl had his revolver.

Without a gun he felt naked and defenseless. All the brush riders through the hills knew he was mining and if they had heard of his disability some of them might take it into their heads to jump him, try to make him tell where he hid his dust. Then as they came closer he knew them.

Old Jake was in the lead. There were three others, pulling up in a semicircle around him. Job, Jake's brother Alf, and a man called Burnsides. Jake eased his body in the saddle and grinned, showing his yellow, broken teeth.

"See he didn't die, Job. You lose your bet."

Job giggled. "Time will come."

Steele stood against the corral fence, debating. Should he mention the missing girl? He hated to bring up the subject, but if he did not that could arouse further suspicion. He nodded a casual greeting.

"Find who you were looking for?"

Jake's face was a hard mask, his big voice treacherously soft. "We been making a circle, Bobby. Started out with a thirty mile ring. We been cutting it, working like we was rounding up stray cows. We covered every foot of ground and didn't find a sign. Not a single sign of her."

Steele tried to look puzzled, not trusting himself to speak.

Jake roared suddenly, "So where is she?"

Steele opened his mouth to deny that he knew, but Job shifted his long rifle until Steele looked down the barrel.

"Don't keep lying, man. You've got her somewhere."

Steele said, "You searched the place yourselves."

Alf spat. "Did you look in the old mine tunnel? The one way up the hill?"

Both Jake and Job looked at him, then Job swung back to face Steele. Jake growled at his brother.

"What old tunnel? I never heard about it."

"I found it three, four years ago," Alf said, "chasing a crippled deer. A false lead, I guess, not much to it. Up the creek past Steele's workings maybe a quarter mile. It's all overgrown, hard to locate."

Jake put his horse along the path toward where Steele's sluice box sat beside the stream, and swung down. He began working on, through the bushes above, stopped abruptly and turned his shaggy head.

"Bring the bastard on up here."

"You heard him." Job jerked his gun barrel as if it were a prod.

Steele's eyes fastened on the barrel. For an instant a wild impulse urged him to jump forward, grab it, try to wrench it away before Job could pull the trigger, but Job's eyes held him quiet. They were glassy, shiny with the desire to kill. Jake had a dogged reason behind every act of cruelty, be it only to force obedience to his will, but in Job Clayborne there was an eagerness to kill for the sheer luxury of murder.

"Go on." The words came down the length of the gun.

Steele turned his back, feeling it prickle between the shoulders, and limped up the path along the creek. Behind him he heard the horses, Job's, Alf's, then Burnsides's. Steele knew very little about Burnsides, only that he was said to be another outlaw who had drifted in here and found a life to his liking, and the rumor that his name was not Burnsides, that he had appropriated it from the Army officer he had served under during the Civil War.

Jake said nothing as Steele came close. He did not have to. He stretched a talon of a finger, pointing down at a spot a yard from his horse. There, sharp and clear in the sand along the water's edge was a print of a small boot.

Steele's eyes fastened on it. For all his hard stare it would not go away. The print was fresh, not yet completely full of the water that seeped through the sand.

His mind raced. The girl must have crept down here to where she could look along the path to learn who the riders were. She must have retreated then, hurriedly, to the safety of the hidden tunnel. But now, thanks to Alf Clayborne's memory, there was no longer safety there. The place was a trap.

Strangely Jake was holding his temper. It was a habit of the wily old man to keep everyone off balance, never reacting two times in just the same way.

"You lied to us, Bobby," he said. "You shouldn't have done that. Call her down."

Faced with certain death Bob Steele felt an unexpected calm suffuse him. He knew what had happened to him, what he must do, and what the result would be. He would not call to the girl. She probably would not answer if he did, but he would not ask her to make the choice. There was the bare possibility that she was not in the tunnel, that she had gone on up the hill, found a dense bush, dug herself into the deep molding leaves under it. There was the slim chance that they would still not find her in their search. But miracles did not happen these days. The last resort was that she did have his gun. She could probably shoot at least one man. She could shoot herself. And that would be at least an easier death than the alternatives before her.

For himself, he was already a dead man. Jake would not let anyone live who had crossed him as Steele had. If further rationalization was needed, Steele's cold carcass was worth that thousand dollar reward to Jake and he would not have to wait for it, risk some unforeseeable slip before the living body had mined out as much in gold dust.

Steele slowly shook his head.

Job's long rifle barrel slammed against his skull. The bad leg collapsed under him and he went down heavily. He was not unconscious but his nerve centers seemed paralyzed. He lay, fully aware but unable to move.

He heard Jake say, "Watch him, boys. I'm going up and dig the little bitch out of her gopher hole. Come on, Alf, show me this here tunnel." He saw the big man swing down.

Alf Clayborne walked into Steele's view, passed his brother and together they climbed the brush-covered slope. He watched them disappear, heard their noise fade. After a time he knew they must have reached the opening. But no shots came. More time went by. Steele's motor nerves recovered. Deliberately he dragged himself to his feet. He had a glimpse of Job's lips curved back in a mocking grin, then his eyes lifted to the hillside.

There was movement in the brush. That would be the Clayborne men hauling the girl down. Instead, Alf came into sight and behind him Jake called petulantly.

"She ain't there."

"But she was." That was Alf. "Her prints are all over the place. She's likely back in the brush."

"Or hightailed over the hill."

Job grunted without concern. "She can't go far without a horse. Burnsides, you duck back and cover the corral so she don't get one there." As Burnsides wheeled his animal back along the path Job told Steele, "You, fella, you stay here nice, cause there's no place you can go if you try." Then as Jake appeared behind Alf, Job began to climb toward them to help in the hunt.

Steele saw something move in the back of Jake, then the girl was there, high enough above to shove the barrel of

Steele's short gun against the base of Jake's neck as she called out:

"Any one of you move and I'll blow this old buzzard's head apart."

The three men froze. Job only ten feet from Steele, Alf off to one side with Jake's huge body between him and the girl. Without even his lips moving Jake's voice came. "Put that fool gun down and I won't whip you again."

"You'll never whip me again. Let your rifle go."

He hesitated and she shoved the Colt harder, making his head bob. "I'll count three . . . One . . ."

Jake opened his hand, let the rifle drop. The girl's tone carried conviction and Jake, like most bullies a coward, did not dare try to duck, to turn.

"Now," she went on, "use your left hand, unbuckle your belt, let it fall. Be careful. My finger's ready on this trigger, got it half-pulled now."

Jake worked the buckle gingerly. The belt with its holstered gun hit the ground around his feet. With her free hand the girl lifted the heavy-bladed knife from the sheath between Jake's shoulder blades.

"You're doing fine. Now tell your brother and nephew to drop their guns."

Instead, Job spun, leveled his rifle again on Steele, and called up the slope. "Your turn, missy. Toss that gun away or I blow out your friend's brains."

The girl sounded unmoved. "I haven't any friends, Job. The miner's nothing to me. But I tell you what, you shoot him, while you're doing it I'll kill Jake, and then you, before you can face back. I won't tell you again."

Job didn't like the stalemate. And he believed he could beat the girl anyway. He moved to turn toward her. Steele

52

shouted a wordless warning, but it was not needed. She astonished Steele with her swiftness, hauling up the Colt, slamming its heavy barrel against Jake's head just behind the ear and even as he fell like a poleaxed steer, firing twice over him. Both bullets caught Job in the shoulder. The rifle dropped from nerveless fingers and he went down, twisting, grabbing at the shoulder and yelling his pain. Steele leaped for the rifle. Alf jumped for the girl. Steele shot a leg out from under Alf and he collapsed forward, reaching, his outstretched hand two inches from her ankle.

For an instant Steele and the girl looked across at each other, then the sound of a horse running spun Steele around in time to see Burnsides driving at him. He raised the rifle and shot the man out of the saddle.

The echo of the shot in the canyon stopped abruptly, leaving total silence. No one moved. Then reaction set in for Steele. His knees felt water weak. It took all his will to stay upright. Only minutes before he had known that both he and the girl were dead. Now the tables were turned about. Old Jake Clayborne was unconscious, his two kinsmen wounded, and Burnsides . . . the outlaw lay sprawled, still and limp.

Steele fought for strength in his legs and wobbled rather than walked to stand above him, to look down on the first man he had ever killed. He felt odd, empty of emotion, as though it were not a human life he had taken but only that of some vicious, attacking animal.

He stooped for the fallen rifle, the short gun in the belt, then moved back toward the Claybornes, gathering up their scattered arms. Old Jake was beginning to stir. Job's shoulder was broken and he sat rocking, clutching it, blood seeping between his spread fingers. Alf lay, conscious but kept from moving by his shattered hip. His and Job's eyes burned into

Steele with consuming hatred. All three were nicely lined up under the girl's sights. She had moved back up the slope a little to where she could look down on the men. She made a beckoning gesture to Steele, offering him his Colt, offering him the decision of what they should do next.

"Keep it," he said. "I've got more than I can use here. You watch them. Don't kill Jake, but if he tries to get up shoot his knee out. I'll be back."

She did not question him as he turned to the horses. He tied Jake's to a bush, pulled the saddles off the others and fanned their rumps with his hat until they bolted across the stream and into the trees. Then he carried the weapons down the path, held out two rifles and one short gun and threw the rest into the stream, and went on to the cabin. He filled a sack with all the food there, went on to the corral and saddled his horse, saddled the buckskin, shoved a rifle in the boot of each. His mind ran over the possibilities before him now, discarding one and then the next.

The Indian reservation was out. They could never make it through the high wall of mountains to the west. That left the big valley, Central Park, that cupped around these hills on two sides.

In that valley, if he were caught, he would at best be tried for murder, and if Reggie Hume's tough crews found him first he would be hung from the nearest tree. Still, the girl should be safe down there, under the protection of the county officials who had no love for any of the Claybornes. And there was one chance there for him.

It would have to be the Park. With all the risks. He made the decision as he cinched the buckskin's saddle tight. It came to him with a start that this was the first positive, voluntary decision he had made in a year. It was like breaking out of water after a long submersion. He was not free. His life was not secure by a long way. But he was clearheaded. The muddle of despair was gone.

He took the horses to the cabin, made up two blanket rolls with his extra shirt, two extra pairs of socks, a coat for the girl, tied one behind the buckskin's saddle and the other, with the plunder sack, on his own mount. He scooped up what ammunition there was and would add to that store from the Clayborne belts. Later, he went into his mine and dug up the leather sack, the slender supply of gold. Then he mounted and led the buckskin up the path.

The girl stood where he had left her, his gun cradled in her folded arms. Jake sat leaning against a rock, a red welt showing angry through the Indian lank hair behind his ear. As Steele rode in he grunted, started to push up, but the girl centered the gun on him and he settled back, cursing dully. Alf, too, had sat up, and Job still rocked, nursing his shoulder.

Steele called up the slope: "Any trouble?"

"No," the girl answered. "I just wish there had been." She did not look at Steele, her eyes were steady on Jake. "It would be a pleasure, shooting him."

Steele grinned faintly at Jake's high string of oaths. He got down, collected the belts with their ammunition, slung them over the withers of his horse. With all of this moving his healing leg had begun to throb with renewed pain. It left him little sympathy for Jake's sore head, Alf's thigh, Job's shoulder, as he told them:

"We're riding out of here. We're taking old Jake along as hostage."

Alf yelled. "You going to leave me and Job here to die?"

"You won't die," Steele said. "It's too bad you won't, but that hole in Job's shoulder won't keep him from hiking over to Riley's for help. Now, pay attention to this. If you expect to ever see Jake alive again, don't set anyone on our trail. Not anyone. The first minute I think we're being chased I'll put a bullet through his skull."

They glared at him but neither spoke. Jake, though, said flatly:

"I ain't going nowheres. Kill me if you're a mind to, but I ain't getting on that horse."

The girl said hopefully, "You want me to shoot him?"

"He's our passport," Steele told her. "Without him, alive, we wouldn't get ten miles." He considered Jake. "You're coming, one way or another. Either I bend a barrel over your head and load you unconscious or you climb into that saddle."

Jake spat deliberately onto Steele's boots. Steele laid the rifle against his head, not hard enough to knock him out but enough to stun him, to send him sprawling, and stood above him, his eyes merciless.

"Jake, get it through your mind, I've got nothing to lose and I'd just as soon kill you as not. The only reason you're alive is that you're going to talk our way past your guard posts. You'll do it if I have to break every finger and toe you have. If I run out of them I'll have your eyes next."

Jake clambered to his feet. Slowly, but he did it. Job swore bitterly. Alf raged:

"Steele, I'll hunt you down. I'll . . ."

Steele swung the rifle suggestively and Alf sputtered to silence. Jake reached the horse and had to try twice before he could lift to the saddle. When he was up Steele roped the man's thick wrists to the high horn while the girl covered him. Steele tied the horse on a lead rope to the buckskin, told the girl to mount while he watched the other men, then, awkward with the painful leg, got to his own saddle.

They lined out then, the girl leading, Steele following Jake, down the path beside the stream. At the bend that would take them out of the Claybornes' sight he looked back. Job was standing, holding his shoulder, rocky on his feet. It would take better than an hour in his condition for him to walk to Pitchfork Riley's. Then they would have to bring back a buckboard to pick up Alf.

Even if Job and Alf chose to risk Jake's life and sent out a search force they could not get messengers around to the scattered relatives and outlaws before night. And they could not return here and pick up the trace in darkness. It would be morning before the hunt could begin.

The lookout posts they would have to pass would be immobilized by the threat to Jake until and if Job and Alf countermanded that.

They should have twelve to fourteen hours' start. And that would be enough.

◀◀

Chapter 6

It was past noon when they rode. They had no trail and took their direction from the sun and the contours of the convulsed land, generally following an easy rise that crested out in the saddle of a low ridge. They followed down the far side, coming into a narrow canyon with a racing stream at its bottom.

The girl pulled up at the brink and let her horse drink. Steele swung out of the saddle painfully, hobbled to her and took the lead rope, holding it cinched around her saddle horn while Jake's animal stepped forward to bury its muzzle in the ice-cold water, watchful that the old man did not try to bolt and dump her into the fast current out of sheer spite. When those two horses had drunk and the girl could give her attention to Jake again Steele watered his own animal and filled the canteens, passed one up to Bella, tied one to his saddle, mounted and rode up beside Jake to hold the third canteen toward Jake's bearded mouth.

Jake used his shoulder to knock it out of Steele's hand and the next instant the girl had ridden in against Jake's other side and slapped the barrel of her gun against the big, shaggy head. He swayed in the saddle and might have fallen if his wrists had not been tied to the horn, his ankles roped under the horse's belly. His eyes squeezed shut and he shook his head to clear it.

"You don't have the sense of a goose." Her voice held the full edge of her contempt. "But you'd better get this straight, now. I don't care whether you get out of these hills alive or not. It's Steele's idea that you're our passport. I've an idea we could make it without you, so I don't see much point in putting up with you if you're going to give us trouble."

The big man glowered at her like a sullen bull but said nothing and when they moved on he rode without trying to hinder them.

"Stay in the water as far as you can," Steele called ahead. "It will cover our tracks for a while anyway."

The sun was now down behind the western hills and darkness was not far off. They would have to ride on throughout the night, for as soon as the Claybornes reached their headquarters the mountains would be alive with riders driving to cut them off. While they could still see Steele took them out of the stream into a small glen. Jake, he knew, was not afraid that Steele might kill him, but the girl had Jake buffaloed, so he left the patriarch under her guard while he dismounted, limbered his stiff leg, then built a tiny, dry fire and put the coffeepot on to boil. While it heated he untied the big man's feet and held Jake's arm as he dropped to the ground. Steele had loosened Jake's hands from the saddle horn but left the rope tight around the wrists, tying the end around a tree.

Jake complained that he could not hold and drink from the battered tin cup of coffee Steele held toward him trussed the way he was.

"You'll manage if you want it bad enough." Steele was

short. "I'm tired of listening to you bellyache. You'd have done your damnedest to kill both of us and I'm about out of patience. Behave yourself, clear us past the ranches and when we get down to the Park I'll turn you loose, but try to cross us just once and we'll leave your carcass for the buzzards. You'd better believe it."

They rested briefly, drank coffee and gnawed cold biscuits from the tote sack. While the girl rinsed the cups in the stream Steele got Jake on his feet, steadied him while he lifted one foot to the stirrup and boosted himself up, then tied him in the saddle again and they pressed on, up the gully now to tortuous climbing canyons in the gathering dark.

The ride had a nightmare quality. With no trail they climbed the worsening grades to a crest, then dropped into another canyon. As the night shut in around them Steele began to be haunted by the fear that, like lost hunters, they were moving in a wide circle, that they would at any moment find themselves back on the main track between the Park and the settlement. In the deepening blackness he could see nothing at all.

There was no moon, a heavy overcast shut out the sky and a wind rose, turning the air much colder. The girl was wearing Steele's coat but both he and Jake were in shirtsleeves, little protection on the succeeding crests.

They had climbed endlessly through timber when abruptly Steele sensed a change, an opening out around him and Jake broke his long silence with a snarl.

"Hold up there. You're gonna get us all killed, ramming around in the dark here. You don't know where you are but I do and you're just about to ride us off a cliff. You want to stay alive you better just quit and wait for light."

The girl reined in but called back to Steele. "I don't believe him, do you? He's trying a trick to stop us."

"No I ain't." Jake was belligerent. "Git down and throw a rock off ahead of you. You won't hear it land."

Steele could not see her but he heard the grating of her boots as she dropped off the horse, and a moment later heard her count aloud, one, two, three, and judged that on the third count she was throwing a stone. He waited for it to land, and heard nothing until several minutes later when Jake's harsh laugh came.

"It's three hundred feet to the bottom dead ahead. I wouldn't tell you except this horse is tied to hers and it would pull me off too. You best wait."

"No," Steele said. "You've been in this country long enough to know it blindfolded so you're going to take the lead and get us through. Bella, let him pass you while I get a lead rope from your horse to mine."

"Like hell I will," Jake shouted. "I'm staying put right here."

Steele rode alongside Jake's horse and stabbed the rifle barrel into the old man's back. "Your choice. Stay here dead or ride on."

There was a long hesitation while Jake argued with himself, then with a string of helpless cursing he kneed his horse to the right until the line that tied him to the girl drew taut. Steele got down, fastened his line and by feel gathered a handful of walnut-sized stones before he remounted and called his command to start moving.

As they lined out he felt a yawning vacuity on his left that continued as they climbed the canyonside, winding off in what direction he did not know. For all he could tell Jake might be leading them into a trap rather than out of one. He began tossing his stones out to the left, but never did he hear one strike solid ground until after long, dragging time Jake changed direction to the right again and Steele's next pebble clicked on rock.

"To the right once and now right again," he called ahead. "Don't try to steer us back where we came from." In the steadily rising wind he had to shout to be heard.

Jake shouted his grumbling answer. "We got to cross Johnson's Saddle here, and on the other side there's a downcanyon worse than the one we come up. Trail's a shelf all the way down. Step off it and you fall a thousand feet to the river. You'll hear it in a quarter mile."

Steele stopped the little train while he gathered more stones, then they went on and Jake had told the truth at least this once. An echo of rumbling, sluicing water grew and became louder. They splashed across a shallow, fast-flowing stream, turned left beyond it and began a sharp descent. The rumbling changed tone, telling Steele they were passing the top of a waterfall, then a cold updraft enveloped them, indicating that they were on the shelf of a deepening black canyon. Whether Jake had cat eyes that could see through the dark or whether his horse knew where to step Steele could not say, but he knew that without the old man he and the girl would have blundered into disaster long before this.

And now the storm that had threatened through the night struck, not with a preliminary gentle fall but with the full blast of a gusting mountain squall blown into their faces stinging as bullets. The horses tried to veer away from the driving sheets, dancing and skittering as they were forced on down the trail. Cursing in a continuing stream of invective Jake rode another descending mile and then stopped his animal, yelling back:

"I ain't going one more step from here in this storm. Trail ahead ain't mor'n two feet wide and this horse acting up he's gonna put me over for sure. You do what you want. Shoot and be damned to you."

Drenched through and shuddering with cold as he was Steele knew that even with the coat the girl could not be much warmer. They could not stay there on that exposed, rocky shelf through the remaining hours until daylight. He got down on the uphill side of his horse, which danced dangerously at the unfamiliar act, and walked to the head of Bella's animal.

"Wait here," he said. "I'm going on and see if I can find a place to shelter up."

He heard her teeth chatter as he passed her, then he passed Jake and keeping against the mountainside, dragging a hand along the thick bordering aspen and pole pine, moved down a hundred yards. Then a sudden bolt of lightning made him jump, blazing over the area in a blue white flash.

It lasted only a fraction of time but it left engraved on his mind a sharp picture of the shelf ahead. It was as Jake had said, too narrow to risk with the driving rain and wind. If a horse spooked a single step would drop it into the abyss. But in another hundred yards the trail leveled off, met the canyon floor and wound out of sight behind a fence of boulders as large as houses.

He turned about, blinded by the lightning, able to see nothing, and began feeling his way up. A second flash showed him Jake and the girl in sharp relief and showed them what lay between them and Steele. The storm was overhead now, rushing across the mountains, with more lightning in increasingly rapid bursts, with immediately exploding thunder. Steele broke into a limping run, fearful that the horses would panic, and as soon as he could make himself heard he shouted:

63

"Bella, get down. Get on the ground."

A flash showed her sliding out of the saddle and she stood at the animal's head holding the rein close to the bit as he came up. He drew his knife and slashed the rope between Jake's feet, then cut his wrists free from the saddle horn.

"Down you come, old man, and move. There's light enough to cross that stretch now. Bella, keep close behind him, keep hold of his rope so he can't duck off in the brush between flashes. I'll bring the horses."

This time Jake did not argue. He did not like being on that shelf with the rain battering him. Dashing when there was light, stopping when the dark blinded them, they hurried down the narrow trail and reached the rock fence as a series of flashes in quick succession put on a display like some monstrous battle in the sky.

The large rocks cut off the full fury of the wind but they were all half frozen and wet through. Steele again tied Jake's hands to the pommel, then hobbled the animal's forelegs against Jake trying to throw himself up and escape. The other horses he turned over to the girl to hold although he thought they would not move out of the shelter of the rocks, then he poked with his rifle barrel along the under edge of the boulders, alert for snakes, until he found bits of wood from flash floods down the canyon, caught under the lee of the rocks and still dry.

He gathered a small pile of them in that lee and lit it with sulphur matches kept dry in a small tin box that he always carried. The tiny flame took hold of the half-rotted slivers he chose for kindling, picked up along the curve of the boulder, and he added larger pieces until the fire was safely burning. In its light he dug for more wood, piling it high against the

64

rock until the flame was robust enough to survive the heavy rain.

There was no way to make a shelter. They could only huddle as close to the fire as the heat would permit. Steele kept feeding the flame, both for warmth and to prevent the rain from drenching it out. Jake edged into the circle of light and heat and they all stood steaming and shivering until warmth penetrated far enough to ease the misery.

Suddenly the storm, as most mountain storms do, passed over them. The lightning was still furious far up the canyon toward the crest as the eye of the squall raced away from them, but the rain quit as though a faucet had been turned off.

Steele's leg hurt from standing so long but there was no time to rest it. He dug the coffeepot out of the dripping sack, lined up soggy biscuits on a rock close to the fire to toast and made coffee from the canteen, hardly waiting for it to boil before he poured it, saying:

"Eat quickly, we've got to move on."

Jake swallowed the hot liquid, then snorted. "You won't get through. There's a passel of ranches to pass and somebody's bound to see you and cut you down."

Steele leveled a stiff finger at him. "That's where you come in, Jake. You call out to let us pass."

"If I don't?"

"You'll be dead before anyone can shoot at us."

"So will you, Bobby."

"What's the difference? We'd die anyway, and at least we'll take you with us. I don't think you're ready to commit suicide."

Jake lifted his bound hands in a prayerful gesture. "Bobby,

65

listen. I'll make a deal with you. It's nothing to me what happens to you, all I want is the woman. Turn me loose and let me take her back to the store and I'll pass the word you can go wherever you want, even back to the mine."

Steele's answer was long in coming as he tried to think of words that would penetrate, break through the old man's stubborn perseverance and the girl backed quickly away, lifting the short gun, saying flatly:

"No. You make a move to untie him and I'll kill him before you get to him."

Steele gave her a thin-lipped grin with no humor in it or in his voice. "Didn't intend to. I wouldn't trust him as far as I could throw him with one hand. Just tell me how we get an idea through that rock head?"

She said speculatively, "If I shot an ear off him he might hear better."

"Don't fire." Steele spoke quickly. "If there's anybody looking for us a shot would tell them where we are."

She nodded grudgingly but she watched Jake hungrily as they ate and as Steele threw out the dregs and packed the coffeepot and tied the sack again to his saddle.

Their clothes still steamed, as wet as during the rain. They were warm now but as soon as they left the fire the cold would knife through them again. At this altitude the nights were sharp even in midsummer. Steele set himself to endure it, for ride they must. They had already lost better than four hours and by now Alf and Jake would have reached the settlement. If they chose to risk Jake's life they would have routed out the Clayborne clan and started them in pursuit.

The trailing edge of the storm had gone over by the time they mounted and stars gave a little light to show them dimly where they were going. Beyond the boulder fence the

66

found the first hazard on this lap of the ride. The river in the canyon bottom must be crossed. Ordinarily the stream was little more than a shallow creek spreading wide as it reached the flat land, but the heavy rain had swelled it into a turbulent, debris-filled rush that lapped over the banks. Steele looked at it with a sinking heart.

The girl said, "I'm the lightest, I'll go first and take a line over."

He had never known a woman like this one. She had a self-confidence equal to Jake Clayborne's mulishness, a complete faith that she could conquer all the obstacles that lay between here and escape and a willingness to try that he thought had been pounded out of him. Gratitude for her help through these last days, a reluctant admiration for her, made him want to keep her here and cross the raging river first himself, but there was an ironic truth in what she said. If the first horse was caught in the current and could not make it, or if the rider was thrown off, a well-anchored line would be needed to haul him back to shore. Bella was not strong enough, nor was the buckskin for this chore.

The words caught in his throat. He could not say them. In silence he watched her take the rope from her pommel, tie one end around her waist and hold the other toward him. He took it, tied it to his saddle horn and watched her unhesitatingly put her horse into the water.

The current swirled around the animal's legs as a huge broken tree limb swept by, then the horse sank to its belly. Steele waited, expecting it to go deeper and have to swim, but with its next steps it found footing, lurched higher and lunged on until it reached the far bank and heaved up to stand trembling on dry ground.

Jake's lead line was still attached to the girl's saddle.

Steele fastened his rope between Jake's saddle and his own and then fanned Jake's horse until it reluctantly jumped into the river. On the far side the girl rode up the bank, throwing off the line Steele had held for her and towing Jake's animal across while the old man yelled his fear-filled protest. Not until Clayborne was safely out of the water did Steele enter it. He had a bad moment when a floating log with branches reaching into the air like dark antlers loomed upstream, curling toward him. It would be a race to beat the thing. If it won the rope would tangle in the branches and even both horses on the other side could not prevent his being dragged down the river with the tree. Steele spurred his horse and as it leaped clumsily forward through the water curled in the rope as it slackened. The log swept past behind him, catching the horse's hind leg heavily so that it stumbled and almost jarred him off. Then the animal limped up the bank, favoring the hit leg, and stopped where the girl and Jake waited.

Steele got down to examine it. A crippled horse would be another major hazard on this impossible ride, but the leg was neither cut nor broken and after walking it in a circle for five minutes the limp disappeared. The leg was probably bruised and painful at first but not seriously injured.

In the starlight they could see that they were on a trail that took them up a long, twisting grade. The east was beginning to show light before they topped the ridge and looked down into a shadowed mountain meadow and the first ranch they must pass.

"Doc Boardman's spread," Jake said with relish in his voice. "Good friend of mine."

Steele did not know where Boardman had picked up the title Doc. He was obviously not a doctor of anything. Rumo had it that he had killed eight men before heading into the Medicines and out of the law's way, but Steele had had no trouble with him. However, Steele knew that he was probably as close to old Jake as anyone in the district, he carried a deputy sheriff's badge and collected what taxes were levied at his end of the county.

There was no way of avoiding his place without going miles around. The meadow nested in a maze of badlands that could barely be crossed on foot, the trail wound down a deep canyon through these and the ranch house and corrals sat at the edge of the trail. Neither was there a chance of slipping past in the growing light, or even darkness. Doc kept a pack of dogs with a reputation for noise and fierceness. Their only chance was in making Jake warn Doc off, and as obdurate as he had been all night Steele was in no way sure Jake was convinced by their threats. He pulled in beside the big man and said in an even tone:

"We'll be passing Doc's place within an hour."

Jake grinned at him, showing broken teeth. "You won't be passing. Doc will shoot you both out of the saddles."

"You'd better see to it that he doesn't."

Jake grunted in a baleful tone, but when they rode in toward the log ranch buildings and the dogs charged out snarling and barking, when Steele raised his rifle and put the muzzle against Jake's neck Jake raised his foghorn voice, yelling:

"Doc . . . Boardman . . . Where the hell are you?"

In the morning light Boardman appeared in the door of his blacksmith shed, shouting in surprise. "What's the matter? What you doing here so early?"

"Come over here."

The rancher started toward the horses, shouting the dogs

69

to quiet, carrying tongs he had forgotten to put down. As far as Steele could tell Doc was not wearing a gun, though he could have one in his trousers band. The dogs came with him, circling, and twice he kicked them out of his way. Then as he drew closer he realized that Jake was tied on the horse. He stopped with one foot raised, saw the gun Steele still held against Jake's neck, then looked to the girl and saw the short gun in her hand leveled on him. He set his foot down slowly, carefully, and said blankly:

"What's going on?"

Steele was about to speak but Jake surprised him by beating him to it.

"If you try to help me they'll put a slug in my head."

Boardman stared, not believing. It was not like Jake to knuckle under to anyone.

"Another thing," Jake went on, committed now. "Some of my relatives will be riding this trail today or tomorrow, looking for me. Tell them to forget it, to go back to the settlement and wait until I show up."

Boardman looked from Jake to the guns. "What makes you so sure you ever will show up?"

Jake grinned. "They need me to get past the rest of the ranches, same as yours. They want to get down to the Park."

Boardman's mouth made a doubtful O. "But once they're clear of the hills they won't need you . . ."

"Don't worry, Bob Steele swore he'd turn me loose, and you know Steele. He ain't broke his word since he's been in the hills."

"Uh-huh." Boardman's tone told that he thought he was not hearing the true story, that Jake had some sly plan up his sleeve, but he did not question, only nodded toward the girl.

"What about your new woman? You going to let Steele take her?"

"Hell with her. She's no good for nothing. The Medicines is full of better workers and a damn sight prettier girls."

Steele had no time for their banter. "Keep your gun on them, Bella. Boardman, get in here close to Jake so she can cover you both."

He waited until Doc moved gingerly and stopped at Jake's knee, then he put his horse to the corral and let the bars down.

Boardman squawked. "What the hell you doing there?"

The four horses enclosed by the fence circled nervously, watching for a chance to bolt past the mounted man. Steele backed his animal along the fence, saying:

"Just putting you afoot so you don't get any foolish ideas. Jake's relatives can catch them for you when they show up. It will give them something to do so they won't feel they had their ride for nothing."

Doc's voice rose in a savage yell. "I'll kill you, Steele."

"Somebody will probably try, but you'll have to stand in line."

At the far corner of the fence Steele shouted suddenly, waving his hat, slamming it against the top pole. The animals inside quit circling and headed for the gate, plunging through in a bunch. Boardman jumped away from Jake's side and sprinted toward the house. The girl's gun cracked, the bullet kicking up dust one step ahead of him, and she called:

"Get back here."

Doc skidded to a stop, spun on her and slapped at his empty hip instinctively, his voice shaken.

"Where'd you learn to shoot like that, woman? Or did you miss."

"Kentucky, hunting meat, and we don't miss if we want to eat. Get on back."

Boardman walked backward to Jake's horse, his eyes never leaving the girl, smoldering viciously, but he said nothing more. Steele rode on to the cabin, a two-room log building with a lean-to kitchen jutting from the rear. He stepped down, dropped the reins over the horse's head and walked through the house. A rifle hung on pegs driven into the chinks between the logs in the first room. He took it down and broke it against the stone fireplace. In the second room a shotgun stood in one corner and a single Colt hung in a cartridge belt slung over a chair beside the bed. He carried both guns back to the first room, broke the shotgun, went on out and hung the belt and short gun over his pommel and mounted, riding back to the others.

"Let's go, Bella, Jake."

With his rifle across his knees he saw Bella lead off, Jake's horse tethered behind her, twisting in his saddle to watch Boardman as he followed, taking no chance that the man had a hidden gun. Just before he lost sight of the yard as he rounded a bend, Boardman made his first move, lifting a hand to take off his hat and scratch at his head.

Chapter 7

‹‹

Jim Gordon lived alone at the next ranch and when they reached it near noon the corral was empty. Although smoke still trickled up through the tin chimney from the morning fire Steele judged the man was not home. He swung down and had a careful look inside the single room and found no one there. The stove was still warm and a half-full pot of coffee steamed on a rear lid.

He took two pieces of wood from the neat stack, shoved them into the firebox, then went outside.

"We'll eat something here and rest a little," he told the girl. "You rather cook or watch Jake."

"I'll cook. I'm tired of the smell of him."

She dropped down but stood by with her gun ready while Steele untied Jake and dismounted him, set him on the stone well curbing and lowered himself to the ground far enough away that the old man could not jump him. Then she went inside and soon the odors of frying salt meat and warming pan bread came out to the yard.

They rested half an hour while the horses cropped at the calf-high grass, then ate and the girl guarded Jake while Steele cleaned up the dishes. Then they were back in the saddle, heading on down toward the far-off Park.

The hills grew noticeably lower through the afternoon and they had an occasional glimpse of the big, lush central valley through gaps between the lowering ridges. At three they were in the side canyon that held Murphy's homestead. Murphy differed from most of the hill ranchers in that he was married and so far as was known he was not dodging any law. True, he paid tribute to old Jake for the privilege of staying in the Medicines, but he was not an aggressive man. He had told Steele that originally he had come here to get away from an earlier wife and once settled found that he liked it. Steele had gotten along well enough with the man and he expected no trouble now, but he could not take chances. He pulled ahead of Jake and the girl and rode into the yard well in advance of them, telling her to keep Jake where they were.

Murphy was repairing a broken reach on his hay wagon and at Steele's hail he straightened and lifted a welcoming hand. He was thin, unusually tall with a turkey neck and a yo-yo Adam's apple when he was excited, a smiling, joking man. His grin spread as he recognized Steele and he started forward, calling cordially:

"Light a spell, Bob. What brings you so far from your mine?"

Steele pulled up but did not get down. He said cautiously, "I'm headed out of the country, Murph, and I've got old Jake as hostage to get me through."

"Old Jake?" Murphy's mouth fell open and his Adam's apple bobbed. "How'd you get him? What's happened?"

Steele told him quickly, watching Murphy's astonishment grow. "We've got to ride through," he finished, "but it will be better for you if he doesn't see you, if he thinks you're not here. That way he can't blame you later for not trying to stop me."

Murphy wet his thin lips and bobbed his head. "Thanks, Bob. I hope you make it, and that poor girl too." He flapped a hand and hurried into the house by the rear door.

Steele waited until the door closed, then rode back around to the front gate where Jake and the girl waited.

"Nobody home here either," he said. "Let's get by before they come home."

They followed the trail as it cut across one corner of the yard and at the back of the buildings saw the corral. Jake hoisted around in his saddle as far as his tied hands would let him and growled at Steele.

"There's two horses in there and that's all he's got. He's home all right. What did you tell him?"

Steele shrugged and lied easily. "Maybe he and Lily went hunting up in the rocks. They hunt there on foot, you know."

Jake glared at him, still suspicious, but it was true that Murphy and his wife hunted small game on a rocky ridge that a horse could not cover.

Steele was beginning to relax a little. The rest of the ranches that had to be passed were off the trail and barring accident he hoped they could go by them unobserved. Another reason for a growing confidence was that there had been no indication of pursuit. If the Claybornes had ridden all night they should be on his heels now, unless Boardman had obeyed old Jake's orders and talked them out of going farther.

So the rifle shot came as a shock, a flat, sharp sound from the timber on the right, off the trail, to snap him tense again. The brush distorted the noise, made it impossible to tell how far away the firing was, nor was he certain the shot had been aimed at them. It could be someone after a deer or a rancher tracking a wolf. The girl swung about and leveled her gun on Jake, glancing past him to Steele, her eyes wide and alert. He called softly:

"Go on, go on."

She did not argue but started her horse forward at once as he put his animal into the timber. Once screened within the dense growth he stopped and sat listening, straining to hear. He had not drawn his rifle from the boot. He would not need it until he saw something to shoot at and even the sliding of metal against leather could cover some whisper of movement he had to hear.

The whisper came, deeper in the timber. Here aspen grew so thick they made a barricade through which a horse could hardly be pushed, and on the rising canyonside above him pole pines thrust up on spindle trunks reaching for sunlight. Somewhere in there something definitely moved. A heavy animal or a man riding, but not a deer. A deer did not crash through timber unless in panic. It might be a bear, not caring how much noise he made.

Then Steele's searching eyes caught the flicking passage of a man's hat through the brush curtain. He slipped the rifle from the boot and rested it across his horn, not knowing who was there but wanting to be ready.

The crashing came nearer and a moment later the rider forced his horse through the trees and they faced each other, only a hundred feet apart. Steele did not know the man's name but he was without doubt a Clayborne. The mark of the breed was plain. Neither was there any doubt that this one knew who Steele was. His rifle was in his hand, the barrel resting across his knee against the side of his horse's neck.

Convulsively he brought it up and surprise tightened his finger on the trigger. The gun fired. The horse, startled by the blast so close to its ear, jumped, and the bullet nipped a tree branch not a foot above Steele's head.

Steele did not panic. He watched Clayborne fight the horse, try to bring it around so he could get a second shot. Steele lifted his rifle and fired. He could not tell where his bullet hit because as Clayborne's hand dropped his rein his horse dropped its head and lunged off through the trees taking the wounded man with it.

Steel was about to follow when he heard a shout from one side of him and another from the opposite direction. The Clayborne was not alone and Steele could not know how many were in the party. He was sure of only two plus the one he had hit.

As quietly as he could he edged his horse back to the trail and spurred after Bella and old Jake. His urgent need now was to find someplace ahead from which he could hold the trail against the Claybornes until the girl could get to safety. Riding hard he tried to recall how that section of trail worked up over the next ridge, the last between him and the long slope into the big valley. He thought he remembered it passing over the crest through a notch so narrow that two riders could not use it abreast. If he could reach that notch before the Claybornes closed in he could hold them there until darkness would hide his escape.

He counted without the girl, turning up the trail and driving his horse toward a rocky shoulder that hid him from behind when he rounded it. And there she was, riding toward him.

He waved a hand to stop her, not daring to yell, saw her rein in and pulled up at her side.

"Where's Jake?"

"I tied his horse to a tree and came back to see if you were all right."

"Come on, they're behind me, they'll be coming. Get out of here. Take Jake and try to get through the Pass. I'll cover you."

She gave him a momentary thoughtful glance and then drove up the trail. Steele turned immediately to look back down it, not knowing how close the Claybornes were. The rock shoulder he had just rounded would offer a place to hold them for a little while, rising sharply on one side, too steep for a horse and across from it the ground dropped in a rock face to the canyon bottom.

He tied his horse to an aspen and ran on to the nose of the shoulder, his rifle carried loosely in his hand, listening intently, expecting riders to pound into sight at any second, but he reached the nose, took off his hat and peered around it. Nothing moved on the trail. He looked up. The rock he stood against rose nearly vertical perhaps fifteen feet, then leveled off into a steep shelf on which a group of trees made a screen.

He had time, he thought, to scale the face if the riders were coming by the trail, but they knew this country well, they might have a shortcut over the hill, and in that case he would be a sitting duck on the shelf. As always, it seemed to him, Bob Steele was out of choices. He ran back for the rope on his horse, dallied out a loop as he hurried again to the face and tossed it at the stub of a four inch branch broken from a tree at the edge of the cluster. His first throw missed. His second caught and he cinched it in, tested it, slung his rifle over his shoulder and committed his weight to the rope. His bad leg made it hard, scratching for toeholds, working up hand over hand, and in the three minutes it took to make the climb his clothes were soaked through with sweat, from the exertion and from the tension of hanging there, exposed and helpless should the Claybornes come to discover him. Then he was crouched in the trees, and none too soon.

Even as he found a place behind a pine, wedging his foot against the trunk to hold himself on the steep slope, a horseman eased out of the brush a quarter of a mile down the trail. He came out edgily as if expecting to be shot at, as if he thought Steele was hidden in the deep brush somewhere nearby. His head swiveled, searching both ways along the trail. Steele could almost see him think, like an animal calculating its chances. Then he put his horse forward, one slow step at a time until the whole animal was in view. It was followed by a second horseman and then a third, whose arm was crooked in a sling, which would be the one Steele had shot.

They spaced themselves out, studying the uphill side, plainly undecided whether Steele had come down to the trail or was still above them in the timber, then the first rider swung an arm and they rode toward the shoulder, heading for the notch to cut him off.

He let the leader come within a hundred yards, then sighted and shot the horse out from under him. The man went down flat on his face. The second in line swung up his gun and sprayed bullets over the area ahead of them. Steele killed that horse too and was startled to see the rider flung sideways in a spinning turn that sent him over the rocky edge to fall flailing into the stream far below.

His high scream filled the canyon, diminishing in strength, long after his body had disappeared from view. The third member, the wounded one, wheeled his horse and drove into the brush, ignoring the cries of the man on the ground for help.

Steele could have shot him easily but did not. Killing men was too new to him to let him shoot one this helpless, mortal enemy though he was. He watched as this Clayborne fought to his hands and knees, then to his feet. The fall had hurt his shoulder and he nursed a crooked hanging arm with his other hand while he staggered into the timber, leaving his rifle lying on the ground.

Steele waited until all sounds from the men on the hill had died, until the small animal noises resumed, then untied his rope, looped it over the branch and slid down, retrieving it at the bottom. He walked quickly to his horse, mounted and rode after the girl, hoping that the three Claybornes were alone, that there were not other parties gathering along the communications web.

The sun had gone down in a blazing display and a half light had settled into the canyon like a purple haze, lending the pole pine and lighter aspen a deeper tone behind the transparent fog. By the time Steele had climbed to the Pass it was full dark. He went through it cautiously but there was no ambush, and that gave him confidence that if there was still pursuit it was well behind him. He decided against waiting there, choosing to use the dark for cover for the remaining distance to the valley. There was little danger in a night ride now, for the trail followed the canyon bottom, too narrow and the walls too sharply rising to let him blunder off the track no matter how black the sky became. He made good time. It was only a little over three miles from the divide until the land flattened out into the floor of Central Park.

Where the two hogbacks rose out of the valley to form the canyon he looked out over the rolling grassland, in the star glow made out the dark shapes of sparse cattle but saw no sign of riders, neither Claybornes nor the girl and old Jake.

For a worried moment he wondered if Clayborne relays had circled and caught them, then her voice came from a clump of rocks:

"Steele?"

If she was a prisoner they could have forced her to call, but there was relief in her tone that told him she was all right. He answered her and rode toward the rocks.

"Thank God," she said, and for the first time her voice cracked under the long strain. It brought home to him a stabbing realization of how exhausted she must be, yet her back was ramrod straight in the starlight as she came into sight. "That shooting. When you were so long in coming I was afraid you'd been . . . Who was it?"

"Claybornes, three of them."

From the edge of the rocks Jake snorted his disgust. He did not trouble to ask about his relatives. The fact that Steele was here and they were not was indication enough that they had had the worst of the fight.

Steele said to the girl, "Can you still ride? We ought to use the night to cross the Park and I don't trust Jake's kin enough to lay over here."

For answer she turned her horse out onto the flat, Jake's animal still tied to hers.

Jake tried to bluster, but there was underlying uncertainty in his growl. "You promised, Bobby. We're in the Park. You said you'd turn me loose."

The girl pulled up, saying sharply, "Don't do it, Steele. Let me put a bullet in his ugly head. He's worse than a rattler."

"That he is, Bella, but I gave my word. I have to keep that good."

She did not argue further but lifted her short gun into her

lap, covering Jake, looking for an excuse to use it while Steele got down, cut the old man's legs free and helped him out of the saddle.

"Lie down, on your left side," he ordered.

For a moment Jake stood like a bull ready to charge, then curled himself down on the ground, his roped wrists in front of him. Steele stood behind him, bent and slashed the bonds, stepping quickly back out of reach. Ever tricky and dangerous, the old man could be expected to lash out with his legs, try to knock Steele down. But he did not, he lay quietly, rubbing at his wrists, rubbing circulation into the numbed fingers. Steele backed to his horse, watching Jake, mounted and told the girl, "Let's go."

As her animal moved off it towed Jake's mount. Jake shoved up, sitting, his knees doubled, and shouted at Steele: "My horse. You put me afoot and I'll starve sure."

"You can walk to the closest ranch." Steele's voice held no sympathy. "You've got blubber enough to last you a week."

He turned in beside the girl and they rode away, hearing Jake's furious invective fade behind them.

Chapter 8

≪≪≪≪≪≪≪≪≪≪≪≪≪≪≪≪≪≪≪≪≪≪≪≪≪≪≪≪≪≪≪≪≪≪≪

The girl said, "Now that we're in the Park how far do we have to go tonight?"

The undertone of weariness was plain. Too much had been asked of this starved, bedraggled creature for too long a while. Bob Steele knew a tenderness for her that he had never known before, that made him ache to help her, but all he could offer now was more dangerous riding.

"About ten more miles," he said. "We have to cross part of the Hume ranch to get to Don Berry's place, and if Reggie Hume's crew is riding tonight and finds me I might just as well have let Jake gun me down."

"Don Berry, that's your friend who broke you out of jail?"

"Not a friend, really. He was my boss. I worked for him four years. He made me foreman only a couple of months before I went to Hume's after our cattle, the night Ralph Hume was murdered. Berry broke me out because I'd got his cattle back for him."

"But you think he'll help you again?"

"It's you I want him to help. I want him to take you to the

83

Territorial governor and put you under his protection where Jake can't get at you again."

"And you, Bob Steele, what will you do?"

"Light out for Canada, try to make it out of the Park before daybreak or somebody sees me down here."

"You think you'll be safe, going to Berry's? You said his crew wouldn't stand behind you at your hearing."

He had been puzzling over that himself, wondering how to approach the ranch, wondering about his reception there with this waif of a girl. He trusted the rancher but not the crew, and Berry entertained with all-night parties, so there was no telling who might be there now. Then he had the answer, an old line camp of Berry's close to the Hume border. It had not been used this last year he was willing to bet, with the anger simmering between the two ranchers. The chances were it would be empty.

He changed direction, explaining to the girl, angling north to give the huge Hume headquarters all the berth possible, and cut the road to Sage. Three miles down that they heard horses approaching from the direction of the town. Steele swung them out of the cart track that ran between fences on either side and down into a shallow draw where a clump of brush would conceal them. Both got down and stood by the horses' heads, hands closed over the soft nostrils ready to clamp down if the animals started to whinny.

The riders came on, a number of them, their boisterous noise suggesting that they had spent a late evening in Sage's single saloon. On that road, going in their direction they could only be Hume cowboys who would be delighted to get their hands on him. They swept past, the running horses pounding at the soft dirt track, then they were gone. Steele let out his held breath. In the silver gray starlight if one of

the horses in the draw had moved they would have been discovered.

They waited until all sound had died, then returned to the
road, heading toward Sage, and five miles short of the tiny
town turned through a gate in the fence onto a trace that
wound out to the line camp. As they approached it Steele
apologized for it.

"It isn't the Palace Hotel but the last time I saw it the
roof was still tight and there was glass in one window. It will
keep you dry if it rains, and there's a creek with good water
behind it. I'll see Don and have him pick you up tomorrow
night."

She said again, "You're sure you can trust him not to turn
against you? I wouldn't want you to be trapped on my ac-
count."

"I don't think he'd turn me in even if he wanted to. If he
felt that way he'd be afraid I'd tell how he helped me break
jail. Besides, he hated Ralph Hume and he hasn't any use for
Reggie. Few outside Reggie's crew do and they're paid to put
up with him."

"Still," she said, "why don't you just tell me how to get to
Berry's? Why can't I ask him myself to take me to the capital?"

"Don's funny. He'd take you if I asked because I stood up
to Hume for his cattle, but if you wandered in there he'd
turn the dogs on you."

She was silent for a long moment, then she said, "Because
of how awful I look?"

She sounded so like a forlorn, hurt child that he laughed
aloud. It was the first laugh he had known throughout this
longest of all his years.

"No, Bella. With enough food in you and a real dress you'll

85

be pretty enough for anybody. But Don was married once, to a tramp. She ran off with a drifter and worse, to Don, she took two thousand dollars he'd just got for a cattle shipment from the bottom of his post hole bank."

In the luminous dark he saw her eyes narrow with suspicion, and she said, "What kind of a joke is that supposed to be?"

"No joke. If you'd lived long in this country you'd know that people have used post holes as banks from one end of the west to the other. They say the practice started in the cow pens in Texas. In the early seventies when the big trail herds went up the Chisum and the other trails to the railheads there were mighty few banks back in Texas, and the old brush busters who ran the ranches didn't trust them anyhow. They'd go home with their herd money in gold coin, pull up a corral fence post and plant the gold at the bottom of the hole and put the post back on top of it. Anyhow, Berry wouldn't help you unless I asked him."

She was silent, thinking her own thoughts until they reached the line camp. It had been built as a settler's cabin and was better than the average shelters used by the line riders on their rounds of checking the drift fences. There was a rough corral behind it but Steele did not use it. When they swung down before the door he walked the buckskin inside, stripping off the saddle, saying:

"Sorry you girls will have to bunk together but this is too close to Hume property to risk their spotting a horse here."

She found a wry humor of her own. "After a week with Jake Clayborne a horse is fine company."

He took the blanket roll from Jake's horse, tore the blanket into squares and hung them across the two windows, lighted the lamp with the blackened chimney and went outside to see if light showed through the wall chinks. Satisfied, he went back in and found the girl throwing her blanket on the bunk against the wall. There was no mattress and the rawhide straps that served as springs would be uncomfortable, but he doubted that she would lie awake long. He tossed the tote sack with what little was left in it on the table and now that there was no more to do here found a strange reluctance to leave.

Putting that down deliberately he said, "I'll take Jake's horse on a ways and lose it. It will be close to daylight when I reach Berry's so don't look for him before late tomorrow night."

She had another concern. "What if he isn't there?"

Probably out of his wishful need Steele had not thought of that possibility, and the idea jarred him. He considered what it would mean, then said:

"I'll come back if he isn't."

"You'd double your chance of running into trouble. It would be better if you'd tell me the way to the capital."

He was about to protest that it would be too dangerous for her to cross the big valley alone, then did not. In the end she might have to. He told her:

"Don't try it in daylight. Go back to that little road and turn toward Sage, but don't go into the town, go around it. Just north of it you'll pick up the east-west stage road that will take you east clear to the capital. Stay off the road, ride the brush wherever you can, bypass Walton and the three little towns it goes through, because if Jake keeps looking for you he'll expect you to use that road."

She nodded and said simply, "Thank you. For everything you've done. I hope you get away safely," and held out her small grimy hand.

He gave her a crooked smile. "I'm the one who needs to say thanks."

It grew on him suddenly that he probably would never see her again, and the thought disturbed him more than anything had in a long while. He did not take the hand. He hesitated for a moment, then caught both her bony shoulders, pulled her against him and kissed her fiercely. Shaken as he was he could not tell whether she returned the kiss, but when she stepped away her eyes held on him.

"Write to me. Tell me where you are. Maybe somehow I can go there."

"Write . . . Who would I write to, just Bella?"

"Oh . . . my name is Landers."

"Where do I write?"

She puzzled about that, then said, "Care of the Territorial governor. Sign the letter *your brother Jim*. You will write . . ."

The idea of the governor serving as postal agent for a man wanted for murder amused him. He nodded but said nothing. He did not intend to write. It would do her no service. Wherever he went the sheriff's dodgers would follow and someone might recognize him, someone might start extradition proceedings. She didn't need that kind of problem.

He kissed her again, savoring the salty taste of her lips, then turned the lamp very low and slipped through the door. In the saddle, towing Jake's horse, he looked back once and saw her standing outside the dark doorway, one hand lifted shoulder high, tentative, as if she guessed his real intention. He would remember her that way always.

Riding across the familiar range brought him a lonely homesickness. In the starlight he noted how high the grass was, how thick. Nowhere, he thought, was there better graze than this Central Park meadowland. The ride seemed shorter than it was and the stars were fading, giving way before the coming daybreak when the Berry ranch buildings loomed ahead. He was relieved to see the many horses in the corral. Some of the hands might notice a strange animal among them, but Berry could invent some explanation. He hid his saddle under some hay in the corner of the barn, then slipped around the main house to the window of Don Berry's bedroom.

The low window was open. He threw a leg over the sill and stepped into the room, hearing the rancher stir in his sleep, went to the bed and laid a hand gently across the mouth, saying:

"Don, wake up. It's all right."

His voice was soft but it roused Berry. He opened his eyes and spoke under the hand. "Who the hell is it?"

"Steele. Bob Steele."

Berry sat up suddenly, knocking the hand away and keeping his own voice low. "Are you crazy? What are you doing back here?"

"Long story. You'll get it later. I need help, Don, and you're the only one who can give it."

"I can't help you if anyone knows you're in the Park. Nobody can if you're caught."

"I don't intend to be caught, and it isn't me I want you to help. I'm heading out of the country, but I've got a girl with me. She has to get to the governor."

"Forget it." Berry was sharp.

"No. Listen to me. I owe you my freedom, yes, but you'd have been wiped out if I hadn't got those cattle back from Hume. Do this one more thing for me."

"Why? Why must I get her to the governor? Why can't she go by herself?"

Steele sat down on the side of the bed and told the story

89

quickly, relieved that Berry listened with growing incredulity. At the end Berry said:

"Jake Clayborne bought a white girl . . . to keep for himself?"

"And would kill to get her back. He'd kill her now."

As if the story made him restless Berry slid his legs from under the covers and sat beside Steele. "How can he get away with a thing like that? I'd think the county law would crack down on him."

"He is the county law, remember. He's the elected sheriff and most of the population up there are his family clan. The people like me, hiding from real law, he uses like feudal serfs. He's kept a ring in my nose for a year."

"Then you were a damned fool to butt into the affair. You had to know what would happen."

"The snake bite," Steele recalled for him. "She stayed and saved my life. I couldn't let Jake get her back. I saw him whip her unconscious once."

"I don't like women, but I don't like brutes either. Why didn't you shoot the old devil?"

"Sure way to commit suicide in the middle of his hills. Don, please help her. All you have to do is hire a buggy, pick her up at the line camp and drive her to the capital."

"Why can't she ride?"

"Jake may be watching that road by now. He'd see her on a horse but he'd be less apt to expect her to be riding in a buggy."

"Well . . . if you'll clear out of the Park and not come back I'll do it."

"Good. I'll give you my word. Now where can I sleep through the day until it's dark enough to leave?"

Chapter 9

Among the many things Jake Clayborne hated was walking. After all the rest of it, Bob Steele had further humiliated him by putting him afoot. It was the height of insult to the old mountain man.

Common sense told him to climb back into the hills to the nearest ranch for food and a horse, but the venom in him drove him in the opposite direction. It was a good twenty miles from the bottom of the grade to the headquarters of the Hume ranch. There were closer line camps where he might get a horse but he did not know their locations. He plodded on, his mood blackening deeper with every step. He meant to see Steele picked up by the law and hanged. He wanted the woman back but he would have to move carefully there. He was in Central County now, not in his own hills, and if the woman told her story to the wrong people Jake could be in a serious pickle.

But the first order was to make certain Steele was captured. There was the reward, which he meant to have as a matter of course, but the force that drove him through the night was the thirst for revenge.

It took him better than three hours to reach the turn where the private Hume road left the main trail and cut across the low rolling hills, twelve miles to the HR gate. It was full daylight when he passed the corral and came to the side door of the main house. A Chinese cook stepped out of the cookshack and Clayborne bellowed at him:

"Where'll I find the boss?"

"No get up." The cook's voice was shrill. He picked up a pail of water and started again into the shack.

Clayborne bellowed after him. "Come here, you."

The cook edged uneasily through the door and slammed it on Jake's third yell. Above Jake, Reggie Hume jammed his head out of an upper window with his own shout.

"Who the devil's making all the racket?" He looked down on the big figure. "Who are you and what are you bawling about in the middle of the night?"

Clayborne ignored the tone. Abuse ran off him like water off a duck. He said in cold hauteur, "Sheriff Clayborne from over in Medicine County. I'm after a murderer, man named Steele."

Reggie Hume had intended to shut the racket off and finish his sleep, but now he snapped fully awake. "Who did you say?"

"Bob Steele, the man that killed your father."

"He's a thousand miles away from here."

"He ain't over fifteen, twenty miles from this spot right now. I arrested him two days ago and was bringing him in. He suckered me and put me afoot at the bottom of the grade."

"Where was he going?"

"I don't know. He's got a woman with him. It was her got the drop on me when I wasn't looking."

"Don't you have any idea which way they headed?"

Clayborne had a good idea of where Steele would head but he wasn't saying at the moment, not until he made certain the reward would be paid him. "Nope. But chances are he'll hole up someplace for the day and try to make it out of the Park come night. If you'll let me have a horse I'll ride on in to Walton and talk to Sheriff Hayman."

"Hold on, Sheriff, and we'll ride with you."

The crew, sleeping late after their sortie to Sage, had tumbled out of the bunkhouse at the beginning of the loud voices and stood gathered around the door, watching. Hume shouted at them to get breakfast and be ready to ride, shouted at the cook to get food on chop-chop, and ducked into his room.

Clayborne walked to the cookshack like a man famished. He was first at the long table and by the time the crew straggled in, finishing fastening their clothes, Jake had wolfed a steak meant for four, half a pan of biscuits soaked in sorghum and was starting on the platter of fried potatoes. Reggie Hume came in behind the crew, stopped to watch Clayborne eating with both hands and finally said sourly:

"Been missing meals?"

Clayborne answered with his mouth full. "Not much time to eat last few days. Too busy chasing Steele."

Hume dropped into the chair at the head of the table, drank coffee, showed no interest in food. "I'm not exactly clear on how you got hold of Steele."

Clayborne had his story ready. He had had a twenty-mile hike to work it out after his wily fashion. He knew that the sheriff in Walton was well aware Jake harbored wanted criminals. He did not know whether Reggie Hume knew it, but doubted it. He hewed as close to the truth as he could, as the easiest way.

He swallowed, washed his throat with coffee and coughed catarrh. "He just comes riding up to my store. Seems he's been placering in a crick way back somewheres. He never come in before, always sent one of the neighbors, but it just happened I'd been looking over the dodgers right before he walked in and I knew him straight off."

"The woman. What about her?"

"Don't rightly know. Appears he had her at his shack and when I picked him up and started for Walton with him she trailed along. First thing I knowed was last night when we'd made camp, she sneaked up behind and conked me with a gun barrel. When I come to they had me all tied up. Loaded me on my horse and brought me down. Soon as we hit the Park they put me afoot and rode out."

Hume was still not satisfied. "Why didn't they kill you and ride back into the hills? They'd have been a lot safer than they will be here in the Park."

Jake grunted. "You don't know my relatives. They can track an ant in foot-high grass and they wouldn't like it if I was killed. Steele knows it. He'll keep as far away from there as he can get. He figured I'd head back for a horse and by the time you Park people knew he was around he'd be long gone."

"It's a wonder he let you go, if he was clearing out of your territory, a killer like that. It don't make sense to me."

Jake Clayborne had not expected this challenge to his story but his wily mind came up with a counterthrust that pleased him so much he actually smiled.

"It was the woman. She wouldn't stand for killing a helpless man. Said she'd leave him if he did it."

Hume shrugged. He didn't care what the truth was as long as Steele was really in the Park. If so and they put out

94

enough posses they were certain to run him to earth before he could escape again. He hurried the men in their meal, in their preparation for the search. They rode for Walton, the full crew of twenty-two men, leaving only the cook and an old Mexican to guard the ranch.

The county seat was a town of over four thousand, large for that part of the country. It was the supply not only for the ranches of the whole Park but for the clusters of mines working in the mountains. Sheriff Sam Hayman was a big man who had started as a deputy and after some years in the second spot had run for office and won against his former boss. A jovial man, his proudest boast was that he knew every man in his county by his given name.

He was just coming out of the Gay Belle Restaurant where he took all his meals when the cavalcade of riders turned into Main Street and boiled along it, wheeling in before the courthouse. Hayman smelled trouble. That many men did not charge into town in one bunch at quarter after eight on a Wednesday morning unless something serious was afoot. He sighed. Fundamentally he was lazy and he disliked unpleasantness. Normally he concentrated on politicking and turned over the criminal work of the office to his chief deputy, Dutch Miller, but Miller had taken a prisoner to Canyon City and would not be back for another day at least. So Hayman, seeing Reggie Hume at the head of the crew, hurried toward him.

Like most of the Park he had reservations about young Hume. The boy had always been spoiled and since his father's murder he had grown more and more overbearing, crowding the smaller ranchers, bullying the merchants and saloon men, literally telling the sheriff and county officials what to do and what not to do.

Hume and Jake Clayborne alone dismounted and started up the courthouse steps, then one of the riders called and Reggie turned, saw Hayman hurrying across the dusty street and waited until the big sheriff came up puffing.

Hume said arrogantly, "You sit behind the desk too much. Get off your backside more and you'd have some wind."

Hayman did not have the breath to answer if he had chosen to. He stood silent for whatever Hume was so upset about until Reggie snapped at him.

"Bob Steele is in the Park. Now."

Hayman's mouth dropped open, then he closed it quickly. "Who says so?"

Hume jerked his head toward Jake Clayborne. "He does. Sheriff of Medicine County."

Hayman had never seen old Jake and was not interested in the stranger until he should have heard what was eating Hume. He looked at Jake's eyes, level with his own, and his chilled down. He wanted nothing to do with the man. He knew that Clayborne harbored fugitives and his deputies had been warned by Claybornes never to venture through the passes. He said flatly:

"What are you doing down here, Clayborne?"

"I come to get my reward."

"I see. So you've been sheltering Steele and when the price went up you decided to turn him in."

Jake swore. "You got no call to talk that way, Hayman. You wear a badge, I wear a badge. I do what my job calls for same as you."

"I don't protect criminals in this county and I don't shake them down."

Reggie Hume shouted in impatience. "You're wasting time.

I don't want to lose Steele. Hayman, bring some guns for Clayborne and we'll ride."

"Ride where?" Hayman's voice was flat, empty with his dislike for both these men.

Hume, brought up short by the question, looked blank for a moment. "Where would he go, in the Park? Who were his friends?"

Hayman spat, missing Hume's feet by an inch. "Never knew him to be close with anybody. Pretty much of a loner. But he was engaged to Linda Thorne. He might head that way, hope her old man would help him."

Hume's face reddened with frustration and anger sharpened his voice further. "You're a fool, Hayman. You know she broke with him as soon as he was brought in for the hearing. What about Berry? He rode for Berry and it was over Berry's stock that he bushwhacked my dad."

Hayman had looked away from both Clayborne and Hume, moved by old habit to range his eyes up and down the street, keeping track of where people were and who they talked with. He said sourly:

"You might ask Don yourself."

Hume saw the other rancher, just appeared around the bank corner and heading for the livery, and raised his voice, calling, "Berry. Berry, come over here. I want to talk to you."

Berry reined in and sat for a moment stiff backed, not turning. He had glanced at the group before the courthouse but had not recognized them. He was in town to rent a buggy, since a buckboard was the best rig his outfit boasted, and he did not want to talk to anyone, to be asked his errand. But he knew Hume's arrogant voice and knew immediately why the crew was there. A knife of fear chilled through him. Under his breath he cursed Steele for coming to the ranch, for saddling him with the girl. He swung his horse slowly and walked it toward Hume, using the time to try to reorient his mind to this changed situation, calling coolly:

"Morning, Reggie. I didn't see you."

"Didn't you?" Hume's tone showed the contempt in which he held Berry and the rest of the small outfits. "And you'd have come busting right over if you had?"

Berry nodded, making up his mind what he must do as he came up. These men knew Bob Steele was in the Park. Nothing short of that would induce Reggie Hume to bring his whole crew to town so early in the morning. He said evenly:

"I was going to ride over to see you as soon as I sent a wire to the governor. Tell you Steele is back, but I guess you know."

He was the center of attention now, of all the mounted men, the sheriffs, the passers-by attracted by the gathering.

Hayman cleared his throat. "And why weren't you coming to tell me?"

Berry's head pulled down defensively. "I . . . well, I wanted to be the first to tell Reggie . . ."

"And claim the reward," Hume sneered openly.

Berry caught at the word, angry that he had not thought of such a reason himself. He had told them about Steele to try to forestall their riding to his ranch, knowing that if Hume thought he was hiding Steele he would be hung from the nearest tree.

"The reward, yes. As short as I am now I can use an extra thousand."

"You'll have to earn it. Where is Steele now?"

Berry wet his lips, wanting to say he did not know, to say Steele had invaded his room before daylight, been refused help and ridden on, but Reggie Hume's hard gray eyes told him this half truth would not put them off. His ranch would be searched whatever he said.

"There's a root cellar out back of the old house, the one my father used before we built the new place. He's sleeping there."

A wolfishness lighted Hume's face and he jumped for his horse. Jake Clayborne stepped in front of Berry's animal, catching the rein.

"The woman. There was a woman with Steele. Where is she?"

Berry had never seen Jake Clayborne, but from the question and the star on his dirty shirt this must be the man Steele had said bought a girl and wanted her back. His impulse was to tell old Jake where she was, wash his hands of the whole business, but the brute look of Clayborne made him shake his head.

"No one with him when he showed up at my place. He came alone."

"Didn't he tell you anything about her?"

"Didn't tell me anything. He waked me up, shoving a gun under my nose, said if I told anyone where he was he'd kill me if it was the last thing he did."

Jake knew this was a lie. That kind of threat was not in Bob Steele's character, and the knowledge whetted Jake's conviction that the girl was still with Steele, but in the Park he must keep up the semblance of a working sheriff. He thrust his head up at Berry.

"And you had the nerve to ride in here. Why?"

Berry gave him a crooked smile. "I was in between the tongs. If I didn't tell Hume and he found out Steele had been at my place he'd kill me. I could die either way. So I thought, if Hume gets to Steele first Steele won't be in any shape to kill anybody, and Hume will be off my back. Right?"

Jake moved his big head. "Seems like . . ."

Hume, on his horse, interrupted savagely. "Come on. Come on, both of you."

"Why me?" Berry's protest was shrill. "I told you all I know. There's no sense in my riding all the way back there with you."

"You're riding." Hume was grim. "If Steele isn't where you said you're going to have some questions to answer."

Hayman hurried into the courthouse and brought out a rifle and belt gun for Clayborne, and called to Hume, "Wait while I get my horse."

"For what?" Hume's voice was rude.

"I'm sheriff here."

"We don't need a sheriff, old man. The less you know about this the better off you'll be."

He wheeled out into the street, lifted a hand in flamboyant regimental style, yelled, "Yo . . ." and with his men lining in behind him, Jake Clayborne at his elbow, drove recklessly through the watching crowd.

Don Berry and Sheriff Hayman exchanged a long, helpless look, then Berry shook up his reins and followed in the dust of the cavalcade.

Hayman stood uncertainly on the courthouse steps, and when the crew turned out of sight he descended slowly and moved down the sidewalk to the telegraph office. Inside, he told the man at the key:

"Dice, this is confidential. You whisper it to anybody and I'll see you leave town in ten minutes."

Dice was small and timid and so took a lot of kidding because of his name. He was afraid of the big sheriff, afraid of almost everybody in town, but he was proud of his job and of his reputation with his company. He pulled himself up with fragile dignity, cocking his birdlike head.

"Sheriff, you know we never give out information except to the proper authorities."

Hayman grunted. "See you don't," he said while he wrote his message to the governor.

ROBERT STEELE, ESCAPEE ACCUSED OF MURDERING RALPH HUME, BACK IN CENTRAL PARK. POSSE HUNTING HIM. IF CAUGHT HE WILL BE LYNCHED, POWERLESS TO PREVENT. SAM HAYMAN, SHERIFF.

Dice read the words, his thin mouth drawing into a round, red, damp O, then he said in a pale voice, "What do you suppose he wants here now?"

"Beats me."

"Poor, foolish fellow."

Hayman looked at him in surprise. "What's that mean?"

"Gee, I feel sorry for him. He wasn't never convicted, wasn't even tried. Maybe they're going to lynch the wrong man . . ."

The sheriff said nothing more and hastily left the office. At least he had cleared his own skirts. The governor was a bear on law and order and severely disapproved of lynchings.

Chapter 10

<<<<<<<<<<<<<<<<<<<<<<<<<<<<<<<<<<<<<<<<<<<<<<<<<<<<<<<<<

Bob Steele slept hard, exhausted. Until daylight. Until sounds outside the root cellar brought him awake and alert. He had left the heavy plank door ajar for air and in a quick, tense movement he rose and put an eye against the wide crack. Don Berry's four hands were talking with an early morning surliness, coming out of the cookshack. They saddled at the corral without apparently taking note of the extra horse there, and rode westward out of the yard. Don Berry followed them out of the shack, waited for them to be gone, then took his own horse and swung it toward Walton.

Steele was hungry and the odor of coffee spreading through the yard was a temptation. It would dog him if he tried to sleep again and there was one person besides Berry on the ranch whom he fully trusted, Sing Ho, the little withered and wrinkled cook.

The story had it that Sing had been recruited for grading on the Central Pacific and afterward had drifted to the high country. Somehow he had found his way to Walton and was swamping out for the Rio Saloon when a bunch of riders from the Hume ranch decided the heathen offered fair sport. They had hoisted him off his slippers and tied his pigtail to a roof rafter with his toes barely touching the scuffed board floor, were shooting close to his feet to make him dance in the air, when Steele walked in.

Steele had not known the Chinese but he did not like to see anyone bullied. He had shouldered through the crew, pushing men out of his way, and slashed through the pigtail before they could stop him. The Hume foreman, Claude Hammer, had charged, and without bothering to waste time fighting a brawl that he could not win against the odds Steele had pulled his heavy gun and laid the barrel along the side of Hammer's head. The foreman had dropped, out cold, and Steele had turned the gun on the crew. That had been the start of his personal feud with the Hume riders, which had climaxed when they gathered in the ugly mood outside the jail where he was held after the hearing.

Afraid to stay at the saloon after that Sing Ho had begged to be hired on at Berry's ranch and Steele had taken him out, talked Berry into hiring him in place of the decrepit cook Don had inherited from his father and who had never been known to serve a decent meal. Sing Ho had attached himself to Steele, his pigtail had grown out again to redeem his self-respect, and while Steele waited in the county jail for his hearing had driven the ranch buckboard in to bring him food.

So with no one except Sing Ho on the place now Steele felt secure in leaving the root cellar and crossing to the cook-shack. Sing was making bread at the big scrubbed table, had just patted a loaf into a pan when sound at the door made him turn. He dropped the pan on the floor.

Chinese, Steele had heard, were stoic, never showed emotion, but it had never applied to Sing Ho. He had one of the most expressive faces Bob Steele knew of. His small hands flew against his cheeks and his Oriental eyes grew round.

"Steely." He had never called Bob anything else. "You clazy. Why you here?" He had learned good English but lapsed into broken speech when he was excited.

Steele gave him the story in quick sentences, then said, "I've got to wait for dark before I can ride out. I'm hungry. And can you fix me a tote sack?"

The round head bobbed until the queue coiled under his black silk cap came loose and slid down between his shoulders.

"Pronto. Pronto. You sit."

While Steele took a chair at the table Sing picked up the bread, slapped it back in the pan, brushed off the most noticeable dirt and shoved it in the oven, and brought a cup of hot coffee. Steele sipped it, found it very strong, but it sent fingers of life coursing through his numb body. Sing scurried into the meat shed where a quarter of beef hung safe against the flies. Came back with a two-inch thick steak, tossed it into the iron spider. Dumped cold beans into a pot. Slid biscuits in with the bread. Brought a jug of sorghum, a heavy plate and battered flatware to the table.

Steele ate, with a hunger that had been building in him for days. The Chinese watched, beaming with the approval of a fond mother seeing her offspring show an after-sickness appetite.

Sing joined him in an after-meal rice wine and was ready to pour a second when the sound of horses drummed on the hard-packed lane. Steele froze, the little cup halfway to his lips, then set it down, rose in one swooping motion that landed him at the window. What he saw squeezed a whispered oath from his throat.

The Chinese was beside him, peering out, grabbing Steele's arm in a talon grip, swinging him around. "Climb. Climb."

He pointed to a ladder against the far wall of the kitchen. It led to a trap door in the plank ceiling. Steele stood rigid. The riders were already close enough that he recognized the eagle wing shoulders of old Jake Clayborne and the square-set hat that marked Reggie Hume in the lead. What shocked him through was to see Don Berry riding between them. And he was not a captive brought along to be on hand while Hume made his search. That was cinched when the troop veered away from the main house, away from the cookshack, and rode straight for the old building, around it toward the root cellar. It dazed Steele to know that Don Berry had sold him out.

The detour gave him a few extra minutes but he responded to Sing's insistent tugging and ran for the ladder. Sing dashed to the table, swept the dirty dishes into a pan, sloshed hot water in, rinsed them and dealt them into place on the shelves.

Steele used the top of his head to push the trap out of the way and swung up through the opening. There was a narrow room above, where Sing slept. The place was sealed with makeshift lumber but was solid and very neat. One corner was masked with a cloth curtain strung on wire. Behind it Sing's clothes hung on pegs above a carved and polished teak chest. Only when he had brought the Chinese from the saloon had Steele seen that chest and he was certain no one at the ranch had seen inside it. There was a pungent smell in the room. Steele had spent enough time in Denver's Chinatown to recognize it as opium.

So Sing in the silent, lonely hours indulged himself.

There was no window as such. There was no need. The roof slanted down past the wall but a space the width of a board was left open between the roof stringers and the crown to let air circulate in the hot summers, the space boarded up in winter.

Steele crossed to the side of the room that overlooked the door of the root cellar and lay down where he could look through the slot, careful not to expose his head where it could be seen. His mouth quirked in bitterness as he watched the men spread into a rough half circle around the cellar entrance, but kept out of a possible line of fire from within.

Reggie Hume raised his voice. "Steele, this is Hume. I've got twenty-two men and Sheriff Clayborne's here. You don't have a prayer. Give yourself up and I'll see you're protected."

Steele said, "Uh-huh," under his breath. Sure, Hume would protect him. Sure.

For a moment there was silence in the root cellar and in the yard, then Hume faced around to Berry.

"You're sure he's in there?"

Don's voice was dry, as if he had trouble getting enough saliva into his mouth to articulate words. "He was when I left here."

Hume shouted. "Come on out, Steele, or we'll blast you like a trapped rat."

Jake Clayborne kneed his horse forward, bawling, "I'll drag the bastard out."

"He's armed," Hume warned. "Keep out of the way. We'll cut the door down. Go to it, boys."

Twenty guns hammered, the slugs splintering the thick planks, then under cover of a pause Hume ordered three men forward. They swung down and ran, crouching as if they expected a volley of fire from inside, reached the door, shot off the hinges at close range then kicked the panels apart.

One spun through, his gun steadied against his waist. For a little there was no sound, then the man backed out, calling:

"He ain't here. Ain't nobody here."

Hume dropped belligerently out of his saddle and strode forward, refusing to take any evidence other than his own eyes. He pushed past his men and stepped down into the dark cellar. A sulphur match flared inside and slowly flickered out, then Hume reappeared, glaring at Berry.

"I guess he was here." He said it reluctantly. "Somebody was. There's a fresh cigarette butt on the floor."

Steele regretted the impulse on which he had lighted the smoke from the sack he had bummed from Berry, and the careless oversight that had let him drop it without covering it under the dirt. Reggie Hume called from where he stood to the rancher hunched in his saddle:

"You're sure he was here when you left?"

"I think so."

"You see him go in?"

"No, but he said he was going to sleep."

Jake Clayborne had ridden aside, toward the corral, looking into it, suddenly straightening, and his bellow filled the yard.

"Hume, here's his horse. That's the bay Steele's been riding. He's got to be here someplace."

Bob Steele dropped his head into one hand in a rush of hopelessness. Not only would he be dug out but now Sing Ho would suffer because of him. Then he looked up sharply in new surprise.

Don Berry was beside Clayborne, looking at the horses, calling back to Hume. "And one of my animals is gone. He must have wanted a fresh horse."

Hume shot his words back. "What does your horse look like?"

Berry said immediately, "A black with a white blaze, white stockings."

Steele's head swam in confusion. Don Berry had led the lynch party to the cellar, but there had been no black horse with or without white markings in the corral when Steele had turned the bay in, so now Berry was covering for him. He could not figure out what it meant and there was no time to speculate now. He must concentrate on what these men would do next, try to think of a way to get out of Sing's room and clear the Oriental of complicity. He heard Hume say:

"Did he tell you anything about his plans?"

"Said he was trying to get through to Canada but he had to rest and lay over until dark. He knew about the root cellar and I didn't dare refuse him. He had a rifle and a six-gun . . . Say, the rifle is still in my bedroom, unless he got it later."

Hume stalked off toward the house and Steele groaned. He needed that rifle. It had been stupid of him to leave it, but he had not expected Berry's treachery. Berry got down and trailed Hume, but old Jake still sat at the corral fence staring at the bay as if it could tell him where its master had gone. The crew found a shady spot beside the blacksmith shop and in the manner of all cowboys when not called upon for duty squatted on their heels, rolled smokes and talked laconically.

The two men were in the house a long time. Steele judged that they were searching it from top to bottom, then they came out, Hume carrying Steele's rifle and Berry arguing with him hotly. The first words Steele could make out were Berry's.

"I tell you I don't know where he is. We know he's not in the cellar or the house. Maybe one of my riders saw him. They're down along the south fence somewhere."

If Berry hoped to toll them away from the buildings it did

not work. Hume's eyes ranged over the headquarters and he persisted.

"No one left around here?"

"Only the cook."

"Call him."

Berry did not want to call him. He drew a bandanna and mopped at his neck, apparently sweating, then he looked toward the cookshack.

"Sing. Sing, come out here."

Sing's head came through the door and his voice sounded surprised. "You call me, Berry?"

"I called you. Did you see Bob Steele here today?"

The Chinese stepped outside, bobbing his head. "After you ride for town I see, sure."

Hume strode toward him with eager steps. "You want to make a hundred dollars, yellow boy? A hundred dollars?"

Sing grinned, flashing all of his large teeth, rubbing his hands together. "Hundred dolla, you bet."

"Tell us where Steele went."

"No savvy."

Don Berry cocked his head to one side in suspicion as his cook retreated into near pidgin. Hume tried to break through the communications barrier by shouting.

"You said you saw him. What did he do?"

"Come in kitchen, make me get coffee. Went to corral, took horse and saddle."

"What horse did he take?"

Steele held his breath. Hume's hundred-dollar offer worried him. That was nearly a year's wages for the cook and Sing loved to gamble. It kept him constantly broke. Even if he were not tempted, what horse would he describe?

The Chinese twisted his head to look straight at Berry, his round face bland. "Took Blackie."

Even at the distance Steele thought he could see Don Berry relax. As loud as the talk had been Sing Ho could have heard Berry describe the horse as easily as Steele could. The Chinese stood by his kitchen door, holding out his hand palm up for his hundred. Hume ignored it, demanding of Berry:

"Think hard, man. If he meant to wait for dark and changed his mind, where could he go in daylight and not be seen?"

That was the tight question. Hume was pressing Berry hard. Perhaps he had been pressured into bringing them all here where they would surely have found Steele had he stayed in the cellar, and was the pressure now great enough to make him tell them of the line shack where the girl waited. Steele mopped his arm over his own sweating face, but the rancher spread his hands and in apparent candor said:

"I haven't the slightest idea."

Hume gave up the questioning, called his crew to mount and shouted new orders. He quartered the valley into sections, assigning a small group to search each, but he left out the Hume ranch. Apparently it did not occur to him that Steele would venture so near the headquarters of the big ranch.

It meant that the line shack would not be investigated at once. Bella was safe for a while unless some rider chanced to think of it and go on his own to look there for Steele.

At last they rode out, Berry still with them, leaving Sing Ho empty-handed, watching after them with an Oriental imperturbable expression that eloquently bespoke his opinion of Reggie Hume.

Chapter 11

‹‹

Steele slept through the day on Sing Ho's cot, feeling that exhaustion was pushing him down through the thin mattress, would push him through the thong springs. He did not wake until the crew came in making noise enough for twice their number, and the perfume of Sing's cooking made him hungry. To the men's questions of where Berry was the Chinese pleaded ignorance, saying only that he had ridden out with Sheriff Clayborne and Reggie Hume's people.

That started a torrent of speculation that muffled the clatter of dishes and lasted through the meal. Steele sat on the edge of the cot, nagged by impatience. He hoped they were tired enough to turn in early, give him the chance to slip away before Berry came back to ask the Chinese embarrassing questions. He had not yet figured what game his old boss was playing, which side he was playing on and he wanted no more risks.

But the excitement of Berry and Hume riding anywhere together kept the four men below wakeful. A poker game started as the talk continued. Ordinarily the Chinese would play all night if anyone would stay up with him, but this time

111

he broke it up in two hours, pleading a heavy wash to do in the morning. The crew headed for the bunkhouse, still arguing the mystery, the kitchen lamp was turned out. Then there came the soft sound of Sing's slippers on the ladder, and his whisper:

"Steely, where you hide your saddle?"

Steele told him, did not hear him leave, but ten minutes later he was back, whispering again, a giggle in his voice now.

"Allee litee, Steely boy. Have good lide now."

Down in the dark kitchen Sing led him to the big table by his arm and put the tied mouth of a grub sack into his hand, led him on out through the dark rectangle of the door. The bay was there, saddled, the bunkhouse lamp already out.

"Sorry about a gun, Steely. Berry keep rifle cabinet locked and key in pocket."

Steele thought briefly of going to the house, breaking into the case and arming himself, but that could only betray the cook. He tied the sack to the saddle and in the starlight found Sing's hand and pressed it hard, then gave the pigtail a playful tug.

"Friends don't come in any better color than yours, Sing. Can you square yourself with Don?"

"Sure, Steely. Berry on your side. He invent black horse for you, yes?"

"He also brought Hume and Clayborne to the root cellar. Why?"

"Smart. He know we friends, you hungry. He know you come to me, I hide you. We fix Hume and Berry don't have more trouble."

Steele felt a great relief. Of course that was the answer, and Berry had had no chance to warn him, and there had to be

112

something equally logical to explain why Berry was riding with Hume and Clayborne at all. He would probably never know, for he intended to keep his word to the rancher never to return to Central Park. He took leave of Sing Ho with real regret, lifted to the saddle and rode softly out of the yard, keeping to the grass at the side of the lane.

It was an hour's ride to the line camp, with no cover except the shallow draws, and as much as possible he kept down in those. There was no telling who else was riding this night. There was no telling whether Bella was still safe in the little building. If she was not, one of several things might have happened. Don Berry could have broken away from the search party and kept his promise to pick her up after dark and take her to the Territorial capital. She could have tired of waiting and started out on her own. Both possibilities worried him, if Hume's big crew was still out where she might run into them. There was a third chance, that they had already found her in the shack.

All he could do was go and find out if she was still there, and if she was to get her started on her way to the governor. When the little building loomed out of the night the place was dark, but he circled it cautiously, wary of a trap. There were no horses in sight but that did not prove anything. He rode close to the unglazed window, keeping his saddle, ready to ride hard at the first suspicion, and called in a low voice:

"Bella . . . Bella . . ."

Her voice came back with no tension in it to suggest she was a prisoner being coached to answer. It cracked with urgent relief.

"Steele. Oh, thank God."

He heard her running feet and dropped to the ground.

113

Almost before he touched down she was through the door, throwing herself against him, wrapping her arms around him, raising her face and kissing him fiercely.

"You're safe. I was afraid. Your man Berry didn't come. I thought you might not have made it to his place, that you were captured or killed." The words were choked, wrenched out of her as if she were crying. But she was not crying. She had forgotten how.

He kissed her to quiet, then said, "Don isn't coming and we have to move out of here, fast. Let me get the saddle on the mare. Has she had anything to eat?"

She followed him into the shack, saying to his back, "I brought a pail of water for her last night, and after dark this evening I took her out to graze. What's happened to Berry?"

"Tell you when we're moving."

He threw the saddle on, cinched it, led the horse outside and held it while she mounted, then got on his bay and rode beside her, keeping his eyes roving, ahead, to the sides, behind, watching for horsemen in the pale night light. As they rode he talked, detailing the events since he had left her. When he finished he said ruefully:

"I thought Don had double-crossed me for certain when he showed up with Jake and Hume, and I couldn't make sense out of his covering me later until Sing spelled it out, that he expected me to go to Sing and knew he'd hide me, but he had to convince Hume that he was trying to help find me. I guess old Jake taught me to get suspicious too easily."

"I didn't need old Jake to teach me. I learned at home. And I want to sniff around this business some more. You said Berry was just a boss, not a personal friend of yours when he broke you out of jail. Why would he risk doing that?"

"I don't know for sure. Of course I saved his cattle when Ralph Hume stole them, but any foreman worth his salt would have done the same. Why?"

"Suppose," she said very slowly, thinking something through, "supposing Berry knew you weren't guilty, didn't want you to go to trial, and was afraid of something you might say in the face of a lynching."

"I don't follow you. How could he know I wasn't guilty?"

"He'd know if he shot Hume himself, wouldn't he?"

The words sent a shock tingling through Steele. He had never considered the idea. There had never been the least suggestion of such a thing. His protest was on his lips when he stopped it and the idea stirred around in his mind. Surely Berry had motive enough for wanting the big rancher dead. Hume had ridden over him roughshod as he did with all the little ranchers of the Park, but he had seemed to take a special pleasure in tormenting Don Berry. That last brazen raid on Berry's stock was a good example.

Then a half-remembered story came back to Steele, in which it was said that Ralph Hume and Don's father John had come into the country as partners, driving a herd up through the short grass of the New Mexico plains. The present Hume and Berry ranches had been started as one, but somewhere along the way they had quarreled and split up. The ranch had been divided unequally, and John Berry had taken to spending much of his time in the Walton saloons, drinking and gambling, swearing that Ralph Hume had robbed him, and gradually having to sell Hume more and more of his land while Hume had prospered and extended his range.

Like his father must have been, Don Berry was not a forceful man. Yes, it was conceivable that driven too far he was capable of the ambush, shooting down an unarmed man. But Steele shook his head.

"Trouble with that theory is that the night Hume was murdered Don was in Walton seeing his lawyer, and Walton is too far from the Hume ranch for him to have gotten there before morning."

She was not put off her track and her voice took on a tenacious note. "I've got a hunch, Bob Steele. A man like you make out Berry to be wouldn't take the chance of what he did for you unless he was afraid of you for some reason. Did anyone besides the lawyer see him in Walton? How do you know he was telling the truth? Was he put on the stand to swear? Was Berry?"

"It was only a preliminary hearing, not a trial. Berry was only called to say what time I got back to his ranch and he said he didn't know because he was with Walker Billingsly in town. No one ever questioned it."

"Wasn't he even asked if there were any supporting witnesses to put him there?"

"No."

"And how close are Berry and Billingsly?"

"They went to school together and I've heard it said that while Billingsly was reading law in the capital Don sent him money from time to time."

"There." She sounded triumphant. "Billingsly alibied Berry because he owed him, but he wouldn't stand still for you being lynched, so Berry had to get you away. And now that you're back Berry is afraid you may manage to get the case reopened. And I think that's why he led Reggie Hume to the root cellar, to let him get rid of you once and for all."

"Maybe." Steele was bewildered by her train of thought.

"You haven't any evidence that it's true, and if it were, why would he change his mind and cover up for me, invent a horse he said I stole, why wouldn't he tell Hume about you and the line cabin, the logical place for me to go?"

She was quiet for a while, then said in a doubtful tone, "You say he doesn't like women, but with Jake Clayborne along maybe there's enough decency in him not to lead Jake to me."

"I don't know . . . I just don't know, and it's too late to do anything about it now. I can't stay around here to look into it, but you surely make it sound true. How can a girl, one as young as you, figure things out like that?"

She sniffed as if he had insulted her intelligence. "Pa used to say I was like his father, who was a Philadelphia lawyer before he moved to Kentuck . . . Well, so you're just going to keep running. Where are we headed now?"

He looked over the rich, dim land where he would like to have spent his life, his eyes bleak, seeing ahead a future empty of everything he had come to want.

"I'll take you to the top of the Pass and start you down toward the capital."

"Then what?"

"I'll come back down and skirt the mountains north, along the edge of the reservation, try to get through into Wyoming and Canada."

"I'll go with you. I won't need the governor's protection in Canada and we won't have to climb the Pass."

She sounded so positive that he nearly smiled. He was terribly tempted, but the chance of being discovered would be doubled with two horses to be hidden from searchers through the daylight hours and with Jake on her trail she was in as much danger as he. By herself, once she was beyond Jake's reach, she should get safely to the capital. He spoke as if there were a bad taste in his mouth.

"I wouldn't think you'd want to go with a man who's running."

"You'll stop one of these days. Stop and turn around and fight."

"Not while all of the odds are against me."

"The odds are all against you only once, when you're dead."

"If a time comes when you'd be safe with me I'll send for you. But go to the capital and wait. I may be able to get through alone but both of us can't."

At least he had one bit of odds with him now. He had shifted the only rifle left to them from her boot to his, leaving her the short gun which she had preferred this far. The smooth stock under his knee was a comfort as they rode the meadowland toward the stage road. They crossed that and he headed in a wide circle around Walton. Eastward of there the flat land began rolling up toward the foothills. Ridges wrinkled the pasture, creeks dug through it making miniature canyons twenty to forty feet deep. If they could reach that rougher ground before first light they could find concealment for the animals.

He did not really expect trouble on the far side of Walton. The logical supposition for the men hunting him would be that he had left the old root cellar long before they reached it, that he would have made all the speed possible, probably riding directly for the border of the reservation.

The Indians were not friendly and if their police found him they would stop him, at best turn him back. But their eastern boundary lay along the foothills in rough country and a very careful rider might slip past them.

Steele kept the horses moving at a fast walk and their hoofs made no sound on the deep grass mat. Twice buildings bulked dark against the lighter sky and at the second a dog sent up an incessant sharp barking. Steele beckoned the girl, spurred his horse to a fast run away from the ranch house. No light came on. The people there either slept soundly or concluded the dog was yapping at a coyote. Then the sound faded as they distanced the house and the night was quiet again.

The horizon was beginning to gray and Steele began to watch the broken ground for a place to rest. As the light grew he saw a snaking line of trees, aspens and cottonwoods thick along some winding stream and he turned toward them, working upward, hunting a spot where the growth was thin enough to let them to the water. He found a place where the current had curved around a bend and a sand bar had built up, a spit out into the creek.

Here they got down and as the girl held the reins while the animals drank Steele hauled the saddles off, then he hobbled them in the grass and let them graze through the dawn, taking them back and tying them under the trees when they could be seen from any distance.

The girl had laid out cold meat, cold beans, and biscuits from Sing Ho's grub sack by the time he brought the horses in, and in the early day he made a discovery hidden from him in the darkness. Bella must have found a piece of soap in the line camp, gone to the stream and bathed, washed her hair, found a bit of comb and worked out the snarls. It hung now tied behind her head with a strand of thong probably cut from the empty tote bag he had left with her. The bag itself she was now wearing, its bottom slit for a neck and slashes made in the side as sleeve holes, belted with the rest of the thong. She looked a lot different, still starved thin but like a human being rather than a wild thing.

He smiled at her as they ate, saying, "If I didn't know better I'd take you for a townie now."

She lifted one corner of her lips. "It feels better anyhow, to get the settlement washed off." She shivered within his coat. "I wish we dared make some coffee."

The sun was up but it would be an hour before it cast warmth enough to take the chill out of the air. Steele rose without a word, went to the edge of the tree screen and scanned the wide country beyond. Nothing within his sight moved, no smoke rose anywhere from either buildings or campfires. He came back gathering dry brush on his way and built a small, clean blaze on the sand bar, got the pot from the sack, scooped in water and hung it in the fork of a green branch he cut and rammed into the sand, then threw in a scant handful of coffee beans.

The girl huddled close to the fire, her hands extended toward it until the pot boiled, then Steele poured the two cups Sing had included and she wrapped her fingers around the one he passed to her, taking warmth from the outside as well as from the hot drink. She shuddered again as the chill worked out through her and a little color came up in her cheeks.

When the pot was empty she took it and the tin plates to the edge of the water, rinsed them and put them with the food back in the sack. Steele rummaged through it, estimating how much they had. Used sparingly there was enough for several days, and when they separated he would leave the remainder with her, trust to stoning a rabbit or snake to feed himself until he dared use a gun.

He went to check the horses, then for another survey of the area in the full light, found nothing to cause alarm and went back to spread his blanket, quietly, because the girl was already asleep in hers.

Chapter 12

≪≪≪

The stomping of a horse brought Steele out of a sound sleep. He rolled out of the blanket, catching up the Colt that lay beside his ear. He stood listening, poised to turn toward another sound, but none came. He eased cautiously to the edge of the trees, keeping within them, scanning the open space beyond, but saw nothing more threatening than distant specks that would be grazing cattle. The sun was well down, it must be later than seven o'clock, and he went back to rouse the girl, get something to eat before it was time to ride.

She was hidden behind a tree, standing, the revolver in her hand. He did not see her until she called, "What was it?"

"Nothing much, I guess. Either the flies bothered the horses or maybe a snake scared them. You hungry?"

"Starved. I haven't really had enough to eat since Red Cloud captured me."

"It's a wonder you survived at all." He rummaged in the sack and set out cold fare.

She squatted on her heels to eat. "Kentuckians are born tough or they don't survive. I was riding and shooting almost before I was walking. It took Pa and Ma and me, all three, to get enough game to keep us going."

He wanted to ask about her family, the reasons for their coming West, but he was afraid questions would stir too many ugly memories.

At full dark they were in the saddle, but where the night before had been almost pleasant under the soft starlight the sky was growing overcast and within an hour the dark was so heavy they could not see the ground they rode over. Then a gale hit, tearing ahead of a racing weather front, cold, with the smell of rain behind it.

The wind brought another sound that carried over it. Voices cursing, hoofs milling on a hard road. He had been letting his horse choose its way, holding the girl's rein to keep from being separated. He pulled up sharply, guessing that they had swerved to the stage road they had tried to parallel without going in too close to it.

The next sound chilled him deeper than the bitter wind. Old Jake's foghorn tone. There was no mistaking it, shouting to Reggie Hume that they'd have to get down and wait out the coming storm.

Steele put his horse around and led the girl's away. The voices faded, then were lost in the howl of increasing wind. A growing roar heralded the rush of rain, then it struck, a driving sheet that soaked them in seconds. The horses coasted before it, heads down, at least moving farther away from the road.

For twenty minutes they were pounded, blinded, drenched, then as if a curtain had dropped the storm was gone, hissing away, across the meadow, leaving wet silence and a lessening of the dark.

Steele's clothes clung, making a sucking noise as he lifted

out of the saddle and stepped down. He looped the rein over his shoulder, felt for the girl's arm and helped her down, felt her trembling, heard the chatter of her teeth. He dared not let go of the horses lest they drift away, nor did he dare light the fire they needed badly. It could be seen too far here, possibly as far as the stage road.

He put his arms around the girl, lending her whatever warmth came from his cold body and they stood huddled so for half an hour as the sky lightened. Then he could see her shadow, then see the horses, drooping and forlorn, and at last, best of all he could see two hundred yards to a row of trees that could only mark a creek.

They walked toward it for whatever circulation the exercise would give them, waded the stream that boiled around their legs without wetting them more than they already were, and found a big fallen cottonwood. The thick trunk offered a little shelter from the wind that soughed softly now but was still cold through their soaked clothes.

Steele tied the horses to branches, pulled off the dripping bedrolls and the soggy grub sack, unsaddled and sank down where Bella crouched against the log, wrapping the blankets around them both, holding her close against him. Without fire they could only wait out the dragging night until morning brought the sun to warm and dry them.

They slept, fitfully, in snatches, but Steele was shocked to find daylight when the sucking of a horse's hoofs in the mud along the streambank brought him spinning to his knees.

His left arm, cramped by the girl's head resting on it, gave under him and he went down, then drew the Colt from the wet holster and pulled himself up again, looking over the log.

The horse was stopped ten feet away, the rider, hunched miserably in the saddle, looking at the hip-shot animals tied to the branches. He saw Steele's movement and turned his head and Steele caught his breath in dismay.

"Don Berry."

"Steele . . ."

At Steele's side the girl had come to her feet, the short gun in her hand leveled on the rider and her words quick. "Keep your hands in sight and empty."

Berry glanced from Steele to her and back. "What's she mean, Bob?"

"I mean you sold him out to Hume. You're riding with Hume. Where are they?"

"I don't know. I lost them." Berry spread his hands, palms up, toward Steele. "Do you think I sold you out?"

"You brought them to the root cellar where you thought I was, didn't you?"

Berry sounded pleading. "There was nothing I could do but play along. That big hillbilly from the Medicines had already talked to Hume and Hayman. They had the crew all ready to ride to my place anyway when I got to town after a buggy. They called me into it. I had to ride and hope I could find some way to hold them back, keep you alive."

Bella's voice was like a striking snake. "By telling them he was in the cellar?"

Berry said hoarsely, "They'd have found that anyway and strung me up if I hadn't told them. I did all I could, pulled a red herring across your trail, lied that you'd stolen a horse and lit out. I told them I didn't know anything about a girl with you. I rode on with them because if they did find you maybe between us we could have got the drop on them. There were only four of us in Hume's party after he split the crew into bunches."

At least part of it was true and maybe the whole story was, maybe Bella was imagining. Steele said:

"Where are they now? How close to here?"

"I haven't any idea. We rode as far as the Pass and found no sign of you. Hume decided you'd either already gone up it or had circled toward the reservation. We were heading that way, bunched up on the road, when the storm hit. My horse spooked, took off with the wind at its tail and I couldn't hold it. I couldn't see an inch ahead, didn't know where I was when I got him in hand. We must have drifted fifteen miles and I was just getting oriented, starting back to the road when I spotted your animals here."

"You haven't seen any of them since?"

"Nobody. I'd better get back to them or they'll be suspicious."

"Oh no you don't," the girl shot at him. "You double-crossed him once and that's enough for me. Bob, what do we do with him?"

She was right, of course. They could not take the chance that he would tell Hume where he had seen them.

"We'll have to take him along for a while."

"No, Bob, no." Berry sounded desperate. "If I don't show up they'll start combing everything around where I lost them. If they find me with you we're both dead, and I think Hume would follow you to Canada. You're a personal vendetta with him, you probably don't know it but even though Linda Thorne gave back your ring . . ."

"Threw it in my face," Steele said.

"All right, threw it at you . . . she still won't marry Reggie Hume and he thinks it's because of you. That's why he offered the big reward, not because you killed his father."

"I did not."

125

Berry shrugged wearily, "Have it your way, Bob, it doesn't matter, but Reggie couldn't get along with the old polecat any better than anyone else."

The girl said, "I judge you didn't like the father?"

"I hated his guts the same as every small rancher in the Park did."

"Enough to kill him?"

His head snapped toward her in surprise and his eyes narrowed, then he laughed, a hoarse bark without a trace of humor. "Possibly, if the opportunity had offered, but I was in Walton with my lawyer trying to find some legal action I could take to get my cattle back."

"A lawyer friend indebted to you. Did other people see you in town that night?" She sounded like a trial lawyer herself.

Berry frowned. "Why, I suppose so, I never had any need to check and find out." He looked again at Steele. "What is this, Bob? You don't think I shot old man Hume, do you?"

"I don't know who did, only that it wasn't me."

"Then where did the lady get the idea? You must have suggested something to her, she never saw me before, never heard of me until you told her I'd help her. What all did you tell her?"

"The truth as far as I know it, and she makes a good case of it, Don."

Berry lifted a sardonic lip. "On what evidence, ma'am?"

"Intuition. And adding up some facts. Don't sneer at intuition. My grandfather was a good lawyer and he said he'd rather trust a woman's intuition than the best circumstantial evidence."

Berry shook his head slowly. "Hunches. I don't believe in hunches or ghosts. Look somewhere else for the murderer."

"Right now," said Steele, "I'm looking to keep Bella and me alive, and the only way to do that is to be moving. Don, lift your short gun out of the holster and drop it, then your rifle, and be very careful how you move."

"Why, damn you," Berry exploded. "I risk my neck to help you and this is the thanks I get?"

"Sorry, but until I know we're clear, until I have answers I'm sure of I have to watch every possibility."

The rancher's eyes turned savage. "Your gratitude touches me. I should have let them lynch you to begin with."

"I don't know why you didn't but thanks for that. The guns, Don."

Berry made no move toward them and the girl cut in. "Do as he says, now, or I'll drop you out of that saddle."

He grunted. "And if Hume hears your shot?"

"It's a chance I'll take if I have to. You have until I count five. One . . ."

"Steele, do you let that woman run all over you? What kind of man are you?"

"She's earned the right to call the shots, and you'd better listen to her."

"Two . . ."

Berry's hand dropped slowly to the revolver grip, brought it out, and for the barest instant hesitated as if he considered swinging it up for a snap shot.

"Drop it."

Both Steele's and the girl's hammers clicked back. Berry opened his fingers, let the gun fall, then pulled and dropped the rifle. Steele walked around the log, picked up the Colt and shoved it under his belt and carried the rifle to the girl's horse to put it in her boot. While Bella held Berry under her gun Steele saddled their horses.

She called to him. "You mean to ride in daylight?"

"We'd better. If Don's right that Hume was heading for the reservation he's far enough away by now, but if he comes looking for Don we'd best be away from this area."

Berry grunted again. "Where are you riding for?"

"The Pass."

"And from there?"

"I'll swing north for Canada. You and Bella can go on to the capital."

Berry's mouth dropped open. "You'd leave her with me? You'd still trust her to me?"

"I'll trust her . . . to shoot you if you try something wrong. She's quite a person, Don, believe me. Mount up, Bella."

She mounted and waited while Steele beckoned Berry to ride around the cottonwood, put his horse in front of the girl's, and said:

"I'll scout ahead a quarter mile. You watch over Don."

She looked disapproving. "Aren't you going to tie him?"

Steele paused, considering, and Berry said urgently, "My word on it, Bob, I'll do whatever you tell me. Don't tie me. It panics me."

"All right," the girl said, "but don't panic anyway and try to bolt. I am a very good shot with a rifle or short gun. Move out and stay ten feet ahead of me."

Steele led off, following the creek east, staying in the trees. He was not certain how far north of the stage road they were now but they would soon be out of the grass, into the foothills. Whenever he had to leave the shelter and cross bare ground he stopped and searched ahead with his eyes before he went on. It slowed them down and by noon they had covered only five miles. But there had been nothing to suggest anyone else was near.

His clothes were still damp and when he found a deep, narrow gully he chanced a small fire with so little smoke that it did not rise above the rim. By the time the others came up he had coffee ready and damp biscuits steaming at the edge of the blaze.

They were all hungry and used more food than he liked, but the girl needed nourishment and Berry was an extra mouth to feed. They ate without talking, then Berry voluntarily doused the fire with the remains of the coffee and mounted without protest.

They rode, rising toward the mountains that rose like battlements some fifteen miles away in a barrier that was crossed by only the one pass, among the highest, steepest and most dangerous stage routes in the entire country.

Chapter 13

《《

Bob Steele had been through the Pass six or seven times during his years in the Park, and always it awed him to approach the savage peaks that seemed bent on thrusting into the sky itself. At eleven or closer to eleven and a half thousand feet high, it was only in the first two weeks of August that you could be sure those mountaintops would be free of snow. Now they were not only white but shrouded in mists as another thunderhead built above them.

The Pass through which the road threaded a tortuous way was really two canyons opposite each other, one slicing up through the western face of the range, the other curving down the eastern slope. Twin streams rising from snow-fed springs within a quarter mile of each other had for eons cut the canyons deep, down through the hard core of rock a thousand feet. The trail that climbed along the canyon wall had been forged out by many travelers. Indians had used it from their first memory. Early trappers had urged their heavy-laden pack animals over the summit on their way to the trading center that was now the capital. The stage company had spent a fortune in time and money, widening and improving the trail.

But it was still a frightening trip to ride the top of a lurching Concord and look down the tumbling rock face to the thin silver ribbon that was a boiling river at the bottom. More than one coach lay rotting on that slope, toppled during the storms that played across the crests.

They rode through the day and until nearly midnight before they reached the entrance to the Pass. Steele stopped them there to water the horses where the river rushed under the roadway, to rest all of them until dawn, hidden in the brush along the bank.

Looking up at the gloom that hid the top, the girl said, "How far is it to the saddle?"

"About twenty miles."

"And what's beyond?"

"A couple of mining camps. Maybe more by now, I haven't been over it in more than a year."

Even by morning the horses were still not fresh and he hated to put them up the grade, but if Hume had gone looking along the edge of the reservation and not found his sign he could be coming back to block this trail at any time, and the old crowded feeling rode him. The footing was slippery from the earlier storm, mud over the shelving rock, the going treacherous. The trail twisted up a ledge against the south wall and the water that had been just below road level when they entered fell away quickly as they climbed.

Steele put Don Berry in the lead where both he and the girl could watch him in case he tried to slip over the side before they got too high, while he might scramble into hiding among the rocks. Bella rode between them, the wind blowing down whipping the pony tail of her hair. Steele watched the sky above the peaks, worried whether their luck would hold, or if the storm would break over them before they passed the summit.

He was weary from tension and because he had not slept. He knew that he should have tied Don Berry, roped him to a tree as the more practical girl had urged him to do, but somehow he had found the idea too distasteful in spite of her suspicions. He dozed in the saddle as the tired horse plodded up the long grade, then roused enough to realize they were approaching a bend in the trail, that for a short interval Berry would be out of sight around it.

He urged his horse, calling to the girl to close the gap as Berry disappeared. Before she could, a rifle cracked somewhere above, the whiplike sound echoing from wall to wall of the canyon.

Almost before the racket had died Berry's animal came plunging back around the curve, its ears laid flat and a streak of blood along its neck. Berry was clinging to the saddle horn, his face twisted in terror.

Steele shouted to the girl, but it was already too late. Even as she tried to turn the buckskin aside Berry's panicked animal plowed into it. Both horses milled for a fraction of a second, then slipped and went over the edge with the riders still on them. One instant there was turmoil on the trail, the next there was only Steele, his high yell mingling with Berry's receding scream.

He sat stunned, shocked awake, then recovered enough to step his horse to the drop-off to see down to the stream. The two animals lay half-hidden in brush at the river's edge, not moving. Then something did move, the girl, thrashing out of the branches.

He almost shouted down to her, then stopped, remembering the shot. He looked up the trail in time to see a hat
thrust cautiously around the nose at the curve, dragged his
rifle from the boot, laid it across his knees, ready, but waited
until a head came into sight. It was Jake.

Steele fired, knowing as soon as he squeezed the trigger
that at the angle he aimed too high. Jake jarred back out of
sight as if he were hit, but Steele had seen the puff of
splintering rock a foot above where the head had been.

He cursed bitterly. Certainly old Jake was not alone. Hume
and possibly the others who had been together according to
Berry's story were probably above him in the Pass.

Had Berry been lying when he said the posse had come
east as far as the Pass and then backtracked toward the
reservation? Steele could not believe it. If the rancher had
known these men were here he would surely not have ridden
around that bend without a call of warning that he was
coming.

It was a passing flash of thought. Steele's next was that if
those above came down now they might discover the accident.
He did not know how badly hurt either the girl or Berry
was. The cliff was not sheer here, but shelved down at something like a twenty-degree angle, and there were rocks, bushes
that could have slowed the fall. At least he had seen her
move. He glanced down again, quickly, then looked back at
the curve, with a memory of what the glimpse had showed
him, the girl clear of the brush, crouching beside Berry's
sprawled, still bulk. His heart leaped. She could walk. She
was conscious. She was alive.

Then fear jolted through him. If the posse came, if they
saw her moving . . . a cold lump froze in his chest. If old
Jake ever got his big hands on her again . . . and he did not

doubt that the mountain king would have things his way concerning that. Even if the Walton sheriff knew anything about it he might not like the idea of turning her over, but Steele had known him before his trouble, know him as too much a politician to stand against Reggie Hume, and he guessed that Hume would back old Jake at least until, or if they captured Steele.

In desperation he thought of what he might do. He could stand guard here for a time, but when darkness came they could slip around him over the shoulder.

If he could hold their attention on him, make them follow him, in the urgency of trying to catch him they might race past the spot where the horses had gone over without noticing it. The thing was to get them started. He raised his voice, sounding frightened.

"Come on, come on, let's get out of here."

He turned his horse, spurred it down the grade at a dangerous speed, and was rewarded with a hue and cry from above.

"They're getting away. Let's go."

He twisted in the saddle, saw a horseman race into sight and fired. He knew the shot would not hit anyone, but it would anchor their attention on him. It did that. Bullets kicked at the mud around his horse's hoofs until he flung around the lower bend.

There was little relief for him there. His animal was practically out of control, panicked by the speed with which it was running on the slippery footing. He dropped the gun in the boot and fought the reins with both hands to slow it down before they too fell into the canyon.

Before he had it in hand, dancing and heaving, he had outdistanced the pursuit. They had come around the first bend in a rush, but they were too experienced at riding to want to make a race of it down the treacherous grade and they were now too far behind to waste further ammunition on the phantom fugitive.

He kept going, cautiously where the trail was winding, spurring over the short straighter and more level stretches. Once he came under fire again on the lower level of a switchback where the trail doubled on itself and he was exposed to those behind, almost overhead and only a thousand feet away, then another bend around a rock shoulder saved him.

Now ahead of him lay a long straight chute letting down into the valley. It was less than two miles to the flat mouth of the canyon where the tumbling river widened, slowed and eased through the lessening foothills to the shallow lake in the bottom of the basin.

He was far enough ahead that he could no longer hear old Jake bawling like a baying hound, and it was growing dark. He had a chance. If the thunderheads that had built thicker all day would block out moon and starlight as the night fell. His horse, tired to begin the day, was beginning to stagger, and he suspected the mounts the posse rode were in much better shape. He needed a place to haul up and rest the animal for an hour. Then, if he had avoided being discovered he could cut north beside the reservation.

He could, if it were not for the girl left in the bottom of the canyon. To help her he would have to wait until he knew the posse was out of the canyon, go up again, drop down the cliff on a rope and lift her to the trail. But again, the horse could not make it without rest, and the hiding place was still the first order.

In his mind he reviewed the road ahead of him. There was

the brush they had rested in the night before, but the posse would comb that first, then they would comb the ravines and gullies beyond.

The bridge. It flashed on him, brought a wave of relief. The bridge on which the stage road crossed the river. It was less than a mile outside the canyon. He wished he knew how much headroom there was beneath it, whether the rain-swollen river filled the culvert. It offered the best chance he could think of, and if the horse did not have rest he would lose it. Being put afoot even in this rough land, with Hume and old Jake scouring the area, was not a prospect he liked to consider.

It was full dark, the clouds blotting out the sky, when the sound of timbers under his horse's hoofs told him he was on the bridge. He turned it around, dismounted and led it down the grassy bank into the stream, then under the bridge. The water tugged around his knees, leaving air space, and he moved deep within the black mouth. The horse was too tired even to protest the icy flow. There was no place to sit down. Steele waited, standing, feeling numbness creep into his legs.

He saw the lantern wink a long way off, heard the men cursing as they came on, and was afraid the light would show them the tracks of his horse on the bridge, on the bank where it had trampled the grass. But they passed over his head without stopping and their sounds diminished, then were gone.

Rain began before he thought it safe to leave the shelter, and he dared not climb the canyon trail in such utter darkness. Gnawed by impatience he stayed where he was, his legs no wetter than his shirt as water dripped through the cracks of the timber bridge, and chilled to the marrow by the sudden blast of wind. He lost track of time, crowding close against the horse for its warmth, dozing, exhausted in body and mind.

He did not know how long the squall lasted, becoming only gradually aware that the rain no longer drummed on the bridge, that the wind was dying, then the stream glittered as the clouds parted and let a shaft of moonlight through. He stared at it dully, hardly recognizing what it meant for a long moment, then he shook himself as a dog shakes itself to limber stiffened muscles, held to the saddle for support and stumped out from under the bridge. His legs had no feeling, he could only tell when his feet touched the ground by the jar to his upper body. He crawled up the bank on hands and knees, the horse lurching up behind him, some-what refreshed.

For a mile he walked, closing his teeth against the burning as circulation began forcing through his cold legs and feet, gradually feeling warmer with the exercise, scratching at the tingling under the two-inch stubble of his beard. When he could control his body again he mounted and rode slowly on.

His mind was anchored on the girl, on how badly she was hurt, on ways to bring her up from the canyon bottom. To Don Berry he gave little thought. Berry was not important to him. He wanted to sink his spurs and drive ahead, but he forced himself to consider the animal he rode, not to press it. He walked it into the mouth of the canyon, feeling the lift of the land, and knew it would be daylight before he could reach the place where Bella had gone over. Much as he ached to hurry he knew that he could not even locate the spot in the dark.

The shadow was deeper between the rising walls. He could see nothing, knew that there was ground beneath him only

137

by the soft squishing of hoofs against the mud. Then the voice came, sharp and tense, out of the blackness.

"Who is it? Sing out. Who's there?"

Steele's horse stopped, whether of its own will or his hand had instinctively reined it in he could not say, and he sat frozen.

They had left a guard in case he doubled back.

He brought the horse's head about cautiously. The man who had challenged him had heard the hoofs but he could not see them against the black wall at his back. The call came again.

"Sing out or I shoot."

Steele heard the click of the hammer being drawn back. With a convulsive heave he brought the horse around in a stiff-legged pivot, raked his spurs against it and charged down the way he had come as the gun slammed echoes off the rock.

Chapter 14

Once out of the canyon he rode carefully, listening intently. The shot would warn anyone near. He could ride straight into the posse. But he did not. He reached the bridge again and turned north along the base of the mountain barrier. There was no way he could help the girl now, not until he could climb the canyon, and there was no way to know when that would be.

The sky, lighter now, with stars appearing showed him the bulk of the mountains, gave him some orientation, showed him the contour of the ground he covered. It also made him visible. He had walked the horse only a quarter of a mile when two horsemen swept out of the brush ahead, racing toward him, shooting at him.

If they had not been overeager he would have ridden in against them, but at the first shot he spun and spurred out across the valley toward the west. They were behind him and his horse was tired, but looking back he found they were not gaining on him. They had been on this hunt as long as he had been running and their animals would not be much fresher than his.

He did not know who they were but they must be from the posse. It was not hard to guess what had happened. When they had chased him out of the canyon they had spread a net, assuming that he would head north, the logical direction if he tried to skirt the reservation, to reach Wyoming. They had spaced a string of watching men and these two had certainly been alerted by the canyon guard's shot.

Now they had turned him. Now they drove him as hunters drive a deer, back across the Park, with the canyon blocked to him and the northward way watched. They knew that he could not run forever. He would be relentlessly tracked down. Not only was Hume's big posse bent on catching him. The thousand-dollar reward would tempt every small rancher and cowboy in the valley to join the pack. That kind of money was unheard of to most of them.

He drove the horse for a mile, lost the pursuit behind him and reined in, sparing it all he could. Then out of the darkness ahead a third man rose up as if out of the ground. A gun fired so close that the muzzle flash blinded Steele.

The bullet missed him. There was no time to turn away. He drove straight at the dark figure. The man did not think fast enough to fire again. He bolted, trying to get out of the path, and did not make it. The impact of his horse against the man's back jolted Steele, then he was going over its head as the animal collapsed.

He landed on his shoulder, felt pain shoot through it and for an instant thought it was broken, then he rolled and came up to his knees, slapping for his holstered gun. It was not there. He watched the horse thrashing, trying to get to its feet, crushing the man beneath it, shook his head to clear it, felt across the ground and found the gun.

The horse lunged up, got three feet under it, but the

fourth gave and the animal collapsed again on a broken leg. Steele's heart sank. He walked to it, put the gun against its head and shot it. The sound would make no difference now. Anyone within earshot would have heard the other gun, would know exactly where he was. The horse lay still. The man beneath it had made no sound, no movement. In the dim light his face was dark with spreading blood where a hoof had crushed it.

Somewhere a long way off a voice was shouting. The sound shocked Steele back to reality. Other searchers were close enough to hear. He was caught, on foot, his horse dead and daylight on its way. Then it flashed through his mind that the dead man had certainly not walked to this spot.

He pivoted, looking around him. On one side a clump of trees was outlined against the sky. He pulled his saddle off the horse and ran toward the trees and heard another animal blow as he came up. He veered toward it, found it saddled, yanked his rifle from his boot, unhitched, swung up and spurred away, keeping within the trees that bordered a small creek. Other hoofs drummed on the trail behind him and the shouts were closer.

"Steve, hey Steve, sing out, where are you? . . . Did you see Steele?"

Then he heard a chorus of curses as the men discovered the dead man and horse. He drove the new animal as hard as he could while he could hear the voices. They cut off suddenly, as if a low council of war was being held. Steele came out of the trees on the far side and pulled the horse to a walk, wanting to conserve it and to avoid its running across some rocky stretch where it could draw attention.

It was big, apparently powerful and fairly well rested from the rider's stake-out, and from the length of its stride it could cover a lot of ground. The problem was, what ground to try. He had followed the creek for want of a better guideline, but it was not taking him in a safe direction, angling across the Park toward the canyon by which he and Bella and Jake had come down from the Medicine Hills. Those hills were the last place he wanted to be.

Yet he was forced on. A pattern was emerging of Hume and his men working across the Park in a long skirmish line to keep pressure on the fugitive. Now that they had him pinpointed they would close ranks to keep him from getting through them, drive him farther and farther from Bella, though he hoped they had not found her.

It was beginning to grow light and he had not heard anything of those who chased him for an hour, but he eased the big horse into a trot, to be as far away from them as possible when the day came. Just before dawn he tried once again to swing north, but as he eased cautiously toward the mountains the smell of smoke came to him on the downdraft, warning him that someone in his path had built a breakfast fire.

The odor tantalized him, sharpened his hunger and damp coldness. He would have given much to be able to stand at that fire and stretch his stiff, cracked hands over the blaze, to pour hot coffee down his tight throat. He veered again like a dodging rabbit with dogs on its trail, and his face muscles drew taut against his jaw.

Time rode him hard. He needed a place to hide through the day, a place to keep the big horse out of sight. A man might successfully crawl into the brush, cover himself with branches and avoid detection, but there was nothing in this area to conceal the animal.

There was the line camp where Bella had waited. If he

could get to that. He could stable the horse inside and find a den for himself along the stream in case they finally investigated the shack. But to reach the place he must double back and cross the stage road.

It took him an hour to reach that and the light was coming fast. He dismounted, looped the rein over his arm and worked across the side of a low hill until he could see both ways along the road for several miles. Three slow moving freight wagons lumbered toward him. The need to reach the camp crowded him, made it hard to wait for them to pass. He was not afraid of the drivers themselves, but if they were stopped and questioned by any of the posse and they had seen a rider cross the road it would put Hume on his track.

He waited half an hour before the last wagon was out of sight, then with the road empty he mounted, crossed the road and lost himself in the low-lying hills beyond. He had barely ridden into a clump of trees when he heard horses running on the road. He swung down, pulled his rifle and crouched, looking out, thinking someone had located his trail, but four men appeared, heading toward Walton, and did not turn off.

He stayed where he was long enough to be sure there was not another contingent behind them, then rode on. Short of the line shack he turned and rode a circle around it, but found no tracks fresher than his and the girl's, and so went up to the door and got down. There a new dismay rose against him. The big horse was too tall to go through the low opening. There was no way to get it inside. He groaned. He could not ride anywhere else in daylight this close to the Hume place. He would have to risk putting the animal in the corral.

He took the saddle off, tossed it through the door and led the animal into the small pole enclosure at the back of the shack and closed the bars. He carried the rifle with him down to the stream and walked up it in the water until he found a cutbank behind a small sand bar. Bushes trailed over it and screened the little cave. It could only be seen from the stream, was hidden from above and the far bank. He crawled through the brush and shook it back over the hole he had made, and found that he could lie full length, moderately dry.

He slept, a sleep too deep even for dreams, that blanked out the gnawing hunger and the weakness of his weariness. He roused slowly, waking and sinking back into unconsciousness, waking again, lying in a half stupor, not knowing where he was, then rolling. One knee went into the water. That waked him fully.

He parted the trailing brush and looked out. It was night again and a quarter moon laid a pale light over the land. He crouched there looking for movement and found none, listening for the normal night sounds and any others. There were none of either. The rustle of small creatures, the call of night birds were muted. The night was silent.

Tension pulled his nerves tight. He had been running long enough, had been long enough on his guard against every living thing to have developed an instinct for danger.

He left the cutbank and eased up, through the brush until he could look over the top of it without exposing himself, searching warily. There was a trick to seeing in the half dark. Concentrate on one point, a tree, a fence post, a corner of the shack. Hold your eyes quiet until you are certain nothing moves in that direction or in the areas your peripheral vision will pick up.

He chose to concentrate on the dim corral, watched it

for minutes while alarms rang in his head. A horse, even sleeping on its feet, will shift its position from time to time, ease a leg, sway, lift or drop its head. There was not a motion within the bars. The hair rose at the back of his neck as he realized why. There was no horse in the corral.

He moved his eyes, then brought them back, studying every shape inside the yard, to be sure that, contrary to custom the animal was not lying in a shadowed corner.

He had to be sure. If the horse was gone it had either broken out or been turned out by someone. If the someone was a chance rider it might mean no more than that the cowboy had seen it was without water and had released it to fend for itself. But if some of the posse had come by and seen the animal they could have recognized it, known he had taken it from the man he had run down. They would have taken it from here deliberately, and when they had not found him they would have left someone to watch for him to come for the horse.

He hesitated. It was risky but he would be a fool not to assure himself whether the bars were broken. If they were the animal was probably still in the neighborhood. He returned to the water where the brush hid him and retreated to the place where the stream was closest to the line shack, then climbed out. The uneven ground helped. Crouched low, moving slowly, he would be hard to see. While he had a screen he walked bent double, the rifle in both hands. As he got closer he went to all fours, then lay flat and wriggled to within a hundred feet of the fence.

From that position he could see beneath the lowest bar, where moonlight showed the packed, bare earth. There was no horse. The bars stood on end beside the gate.

Gut empty he began a wary backing away. Not until he

was within the creek brush did he stand up, and a weakness in his knees made him hold to the bushes for support. He still did not know whether anyone was on watch, had possibly seen him and this time been more careful about attacking him. There might be whispered orders now, men sent slipping both ways along the stream to cut it and search toward him.

One thing was crystal clear to mock him. He was on foot, without food, in the center of a hostile valley. If they got a glimpse of him they could ride him down. Hunger would drive him into their hands. If he were to have any hope at all he must have a horse.

He thought of those at Don Berry's ranch, but that was a night and a day's walk away. The Hume spread was much closer. His mouth twisted in a bitter, sardonic line at the irony of trying for a horse belonging to Reggie Hume.

There was no other choice. It was five miles to the RH headquarters and he had no idea what time it was. He began walking, cutting across the wide pasture, guided by memory. He kept a dogged pace, with a horseman's hatred of walking and his boots making it no easier. He was alert for sounds, ready to drop flat in the deep grass, turning often to look at his back trail.

Light was beginning to line the eastern horizon when he made out the dark bulks of the weathered buildings. The main house faced east, separated by a quarter mile from the bunkhouse, blacksmith shop and cookshack. He gave it a wide berth, remembering that Reggie's father had usually had a few dogs. Once beyond that he saw a light already glowing in the cookhouse window. He stopped to watch it but no one moved outside. The corral was beyond, with the blacksmith shop, and he recalled from his earlier visit a rack there where the saddles were left in good weather.

His back, his palms were wet with sweat by the time he made the rack. He wiped his hands on his trousers legs, picked up a saddle and bridle and carried them to the corral gate, heaved them through, took the coil of braided rope from the horn and dallied out a loop.

The horses, more than twenty of them, shifted in suspicion, circling away from him. He picked out a big black, a deep-chested animal, the largest in the corral. The animal seemed to sense that he had been singled out and veered away, trying to put the other animals between him and the man with the rope. Steele took time to be careful, sure of his throw. When he made it the loop sailed over the other animals and snagged around the black's neck.

The horse was old at the game and too well broken to fight a rope. He stood trembling while Steele walked to him taking up the rope hand over hand, then stroked the neck to reassure him. Steele walked him to the fence, put on the bridle and saddle, shoved his gun in the boot, lowered the gate poles and swung up.

A dog at the main house began barking, then a second and third. Steele circled the corral once, fanning the remuda out through the gate, taking a bleak satisfaction in seeing them scatter, running off. Then he lay along the black's neck and spurred diagonally across the yard past the cookshack where a startled Chinese face looked out at him, past the bunkhouse as the door slammed open and men in long underwear spilled out.

One stopped long enough to snatch up a gun and fire. The bullets went wide as Steele dodged in his direction, bent low against the horse and drove out, headed once more toward the stage road.

Chapter 15

<<<<<<<<<<<<<<<<<<<<<<<<<<<<<<<<<<<<<<<<<<<<<<<<<<

Once out of range he looked back. Men were running about the yard in their red flannels. It would have been a funny sight except that the horses had not gone far and some were now cropping the deep grass around the main house. The crew were catching these up, throwing saddles on, swinging up bare-foot to gather in the animals farther away.

Old Jake Clayborne and Reggie Hume stood on the porch looking toward him. Jake was bawling something but he could not hear the words. He had only the time it would take them to dress and mount as a head start, and they would not dawdle over that.

He gave his attention to the black and the ground it was charging over. They were headed west, toward Hume's closest neighbor, the Flying A, and as he came in sight of the buildings across the broad, level meadow several men rode out from them, spreading to cut him off.

He turned northwest and was distancing the riders, but within three miles another group swept out of a line of trees directly ahead of him.

He swung the black again, due north, and a nausea gorged

him. He knew now how Hume had planned, covering all of his possible moves, blocking him out of the Pass canyon, cutting off the routes past the Indian reservation, and, in case he tried to stay in the Park, Reggie had sent messengers through the big valley to call up the other ranchers. Like cowboys in a roundup combing the brakes for stray cattle they were out in a wide circle and closing toward its center.

To stay alive he had to break through. He had not seen the Hume crew for half an hour but they were behind him and they would come. There was one slim chance left. The canyon into the Medicine Hills. There might be men watching that, but he thought Hume would not waste riders there, on the entrance to a territory he could be expected to avoid like a plague.

Was it a choice at all? He had come out of the hills with Jake as hostage, but alone what chance had he of passing through the network of Jake's kinfolk and their clan-wide communications system? There was no reason to believe he could, but he was past reason. He was only running, being run.

He heard shouting and looked back. Riders were pounding toward him at a distance, twenty or thirty of them. He spurred into the canyon and began to climb, driving the black, knowing it could not keep up the pace all day.

He got by the lower ranches that were back from the trail, topped the first ridge at noon and dropped into the draw beyond. In the bottom he stopped at the stream to let the horse drink, then started on the second climb. He was halfway up the looping road when the crowd chasing him came over the lower ridge.

His body tensed against a shot in the back. He was within range and for the next hundred and fifty feet his path lay in a straight line with no cover on either side. He lay along the black's neck and spurred it cruelly, bewildered when he crossed the open space and dashed around a bend and no one had fired.

He did not know that Dutch Miller, Sheriff Sam Hayman's deputy, back from delivering his prisoner, had heard of Hume's turning out his crew, had intercepted it and laid down the law. Dutch lived up to his name with a bulldog stubbornness and a dogged, relentless pursuit of the promises he made. And he had made Hume a promise.

"You kill Steele before he's tried and I'll see the governor calls out the militia. You will be tried for murder and so will every man who rides with you."

Hume had tried his arrogance, had ordered Miller escorted back to town, and the deputy had told him:

"Do that, Reggie, and even Sam will get on his feet. He can't afford to let you get away with this. He'd never be elected again."

And Jake Clayborne had done a surprising thing. Since he had learned how important it was to Hume to see Steele caught it had occurred to him that the fugitive would be worth much more than the thousand dollars offered, and here was a way presented for him to gouge as much as he could.

"I vote with the deputy," he announced. "Man's got a right to a trial no matter what he's done. But first we got to catch him."

"Alive," Dutch said. "We will take him alive and return him to jail . . . and Reggie, if he's lynched, what I said before still goes. You'll get yourself and your whole crew hung."

Reggie Hume had heard the uncertain growling of the men who rode for him. Loyalty was one thing, but they were not ready to put their heads in a noose for this unpopular boss. And Reggie had backed down, sneering:

"All right, we'll do it your way, Deputy, and maybe I'll like it better, have time to watch him sweat in that cell and know he's going to be voted guilty, give him time to enjoy looking forward to hanging. Now just tell me where we find him."

Jake Clayborne laughed. "With the deputy here riding, turn out the whole valley, throw a line across it and push him north. Leave the Medicines open. If we don't get him before then he'll just have to take to the hills, and a flea can't go through there without my people grabbing him."

Dutch Miller's agate-hard eyes turned to old Jake. "I've heard enough stories about you that I don't like you, Clayborne. You'd better get word up there that Steele is to be taken and held. Not killed. Not wounded. Only held. Is that clear?"

"Of course, of course." Jake was more than willing. Alive Bob Steele was now a gold mine for the Sheriff of Medicine County, and a rider carrying a signal flag was sent ahead to touch the spider web, deliver the word to expect Bob Steele and hold him.

Steele pulled the heaving black into the Murphy yard and saw Lily come out of the door, pressing her hands against her face. As he threw himself off the animal and ran toward him she called:

"Oh, Bob, Bob, you shouldn't have . . ."

He cut her off, sounding breathless. "I need a horse, Lily. Where's Murph?"

"Back in Bennet Canyon. He thinks maybe there's color in the stream and . . ."

"I don't want to involve you people." Steele spoke in a rush. "But the black has had it and there's a big posse on my heels. I've got to have a horse." He brought out the small sack of gold dust from his claim and pushed it into her hands. "For the appaloosa. I'll leave the black. Chances are they'll take it, but don't try to hide it. Now, go on up with Murph and stay there unless they rout you out. If they do, you haven't seen me, you've been up there all morning."

She opened her mouth to say something, but he whirled her around and gave her a gentle shove, saying, "Hurry," and she ran around the cabin. He ripped the saddle off the black, hearing her boots clatter on the hillside rocks. He did not put the black in the corral. It was too tired to wander far and the story that the Murphys had not seen him would be more credible if the animal was found grazing outside. He ran to the corral, caught up the painted horse, threw the saddle on and swung up, spurring the animal out of the enclosure.

The horse had been corralled for several days and wanted to run. Steele did not curb it, and now he was outrunning the men behind whose mounts would be tiring. He passed Jim Gordon's without seeing him and raced on. At Doc Boardman's he would take another horse, even at gunpoint.

It would be dark when he left Boardman's and he could ride through the night, maybe go undiscovered, maybe, just maybe, reach the border of the reservation. If he made it that far he would ride to the agency, not try to hide from the alert Indian police, and make a plea for safe-conduct through their territory, try to convince them of his innocence.

With that desperate hope he rode through the afternoon and the deep draw was in shadow as he approached Boardman's line. He did not see the man who yelled from the clump of aspen at the roadside.

"Pull up or I'll drop you out of the saddle."

Doc Boardman's voice. The man he had planned to come on by surprise, to hold a gun on while he changed horses.

Now it was the other way around. By instinct he crouched low in the saddle, slammed his spurs into the tiring animal and felt its forward lunge. Boardman's rifle cracked. The horse quivered, stumbled, made two more leaps, then fell, twisting, its rear legs collapsing under it.

Steele was thrown to the side, landing hard on the rocks at the edge of the trail, lying stunned, unable to move for long minutes. When his head quit whirling enough to realize the situation he dragged himself to his hands and knees and found himself looking down on Boardman's big, broken boots.

"I promised I'd kill you, remember?" The voice above him was filled with satisfaction.

So this was where it would end, the long year, the long chase. A strange relief flooded through Steele. The running was over. Exhaustion would soon be over. He would be beyond trouble. He stayed as he was, not trying to get to his feet, waiting for Boardman's bullet.

Boardman said, "Get up."

Steele put all the strength he had left into forcing his legs to raise him, sustain him, and stood, his hands slack at his sides, his face wooden.

Boardman nodded at Steele's waist. "Where's your gun?"

Steele looked down at the empty holster, looked at the trail between himself and the dead horse where the gun had fallen and made a limp gesture toward it. Boardman backed away, squatted, keeping his rifle trained on Steele, and picked up the gun, shoving it under his belt, backed to the horse, pulled Steele's rifle from the boot and threw it into the trees.

Steele wished the man would shoot, get it over with, but instead Boardman said:

"Jake's woman. Where is she?"

The question hit like a dousing of ice water. Unconsciously Steele had begun to assume the girl was dead. It had been so long since she fell and, with no one to help her, how could she survive? But of one thing he was certain. If she was alive she had not given up, she was still fighting. No matter the odds stacked against her she would never quit.

A deep flush made his face burn. She had told him that he would stop running some day. He had not, until he was caught. It was as if she was there watching him, urging him, and suddenly his jaw tightened.

He was still alive. He would not betray her trust even though she would never know it. It made no difference whether Boardman killed him here or he died at old Jake's hands or at the end of a rope, but he was not dead yet. Why should he give up while there was breath in his body?

"I don't know," he answered Boardman, "but Jake won't thank you for killing me. He wants that pleasure for himself, and he's not more than three or four miles behind me."

One corner of Boardman's mouth pulled up in a crooked smile. "Yep. I heard. I been watching for you. Just don't be too sure I don't have to shoot you in self-defense though."

He shouldn't be surprised, Steele thought. He should have known old Jake would close this mouth of the sack on him. And in panic he had ridden straight into the trap. The knowledge caused some alchemy in Steele.

He turned his back on Boardman, walked to a boulder, sat down on it and crossed his legs. Suddenly he was not afraid any longer. It was the first time he had been free of fear since the day he was arrested as the murderer of Ralph Hume. His face relaxed into a smile, not of amusement but in relief at the loss of fear. He had died a thousand deaths in his imagination but he was not yet buried. And now he could look at death's face without dread.

Boardman sank onto another rock, the rifle across his knees trained on Steele, and sounded puzzled. "What's so damn funny?"

Steele's smile widened. "Me. I just found out I can face reality when I finally discovered what it is. It's uncertainty that drives a man crazy."

Boardman was not a thinking man, had no idea what Steele was saying. He grunted. "You've blown your stack."

"Maybe," Bob Steele said. "Maybe . . ."

It was dark by the time the posse came. Boardman had built a fire in the trail for light and the riders carried a lantern that Steele watched flicker on and off as trees and bends in the trail blocked it out.

Old Jake rode in the lead with Reggie Hume and Dutch Miller, calling ahead: "Nice going, Doc."

Boardman stood up, grinning, still covering Steele, as Clayborne rode into the circle of firelight and looked at the man on the rock, saying:

"Well, Bobby, well. You came back to us." He sounded as if he were welcoming a brother.

Steele did not answer, did not move, simply looked at Jake without expression. Reggie Hume crowded his horse past Jake, close to Steele, and his hatred of Don Berry's old foreman made his voice shake.

"Stand up, you."

Steele took a long moment to study the savage face, then slowly came to his feet. In a furious jerk Hume pulled his short gun. Jake cried a sharp warning to him, but Hume did not shoot. He bent down in his saddle and raked the heavy barrel across Steele's cheek, opening it to the bone.

Steele fell down and lay dazed, still without fear. It was as if that part of his brain that commanded fear had been removed.

Dutch Miller's gun was in his hand covering the rancher. "Hume," he warned, "no more of that. Give me that gun."

With his full crew ranged around the fire Hume hesitated, but a look at Miller's burning eyes pursuaded him. He backed the horse and passed the gun to the deputy.

Old Jake had dropped out of his saddle, was lifting Steele, propping him against the boulder, bawling over his shoulder; "You let my prisoner alone."

"Your prisoner?" Hume's voice was almost a yell.

Jake's head bobbed. "My prisoner. You ain't in the Park now, you're in Medicine County. I'm sheriff here and I'm all the law there is."

Hume's head swiveled to Dutch Miller. "What's this? Steele's wanted in the Park for murder."

Miller's eyes swung from Hume to Jake and back, and one corner of his tight mouth twitched. "He's captured in Clayborne's county. Maybe he's wanted here too."

"Damn right he is," said Jake.

Hume swelled, unable to speak, his face black with anger and new frustration. Finally he managed in a strangled tone: "Then you don't get that reward."

Jake ignored him, lifting Steele to his feet, holding him from falling again. "Bobby, Bobby, you just tell me where she is and I'll give you a running start and clearance through the reservation."

"Oh no." Dutch Miller's words came fast and hard. "Try that and this whole crew will take you back to the Park charged with aiding and abetting an escape."

156

Jake did not even look at him. He sent a piercing whistle through the dark ravine and was answered by a chorus of like whistles that indicated upward of a hundred unseen Claybornes watching from the brush.

"Think I've got you outmanned, Deputy. Start something if you want to find out. Now, Bobby, tell me."

Steele's eyes were out of focus, giving him a double picture of the big mountain man, and his face burned with pain. He mumbled through cut lips, "I don't know." Talking made him retch and spit blood.

Miller said nothing more, waiting to see what Steele would do under Jake's pressure. Jake's voice still cajoled but now with an underlying threat. "One more chance, Bobby. One last chance. Where is she?"

Steele shook his head. It felt as if the matter inside was revolving in liquid. It was most likely that she lay dead in the canyon bottom, but even so he would not betray her, no matter what it meant for him.

Jake let go of Steele and Steele's rubber legs gave under him, dropping him at Jake's feet. Clayborne drew back a boot and kicked Steele under the chin. Steele did not even hear Dutch Miller's barked command, he was mercifully out cold.

Jake stepped back at Miller's order, cursing the man on the ground, then abruptly switched his attention back to Hume.

"I want that woman bad . . . bad, Hume. How bad do you want this killer?"

"A thousand dollar's worth." Hume leaned forward eagerly.

Jake shook his shaggy head. "He's worth more than that to me."

Hume licked his thin lips, knowing he was being held up but wanting Steele too much to argue. "All right. Two."

"Three," said Jake.

"Damn you, Clayborne. Three and no more."

"Done." Jake would give them Steele, and maybe before he hung he could bargain the girl out of Steele.

◄◄

Outside the darkness was oppressive over Walton's main street. The courthouse was fairly new but already the bugs were thick in the cells that flanked the sheriff's office. Bob Steele shifted restlessly on the hard bunk, unable to sleep.

It was a week since he had been brought down out of the Medicines, roped on a horse led by Dutch Miller with Jake Clayborne, Reggie Hume, and the RH crew at his back. He had not expected to reach the town, but somehow Miller had kept them off him, and once locked in the cell he had waited for the lynching he was certain lay ahead.

Tempers that had cooled somewhat during his months in the hills had flared again in the search for him, and Reggie Hume had only to suggest that his foreman take the crew to town, buy enough liquor for the men in the saloons and a mob would soon storm the jail. Instead, on his second day there Reggie came to see him alone to bait him through the grilled door.

"We don't have to lynch you, Steele. I don't want you lynched now. I don't want you off the hook that easy, that quick. You sit here and sweat. I want to watch you die a hundred deaths before the jury brings in its verdict and the judge sentences you to hang. I want to see you cry and crawl."

Steele turned his back to conceal his twisted smile. So he was to be killed by fear. Once Hume could have brought it off, but no longer. The boughten woman had taught him a brand of courage that he had not known could be. He waited until Hume tired of his game and left, then called to Sheriff Hayman's second deputy who sat half asleep with his chair tilted against the office wall.

"Jesse, how about a cigarette?"

The deputy rose, grumbling.

"And you might bring me a cup of that lye you've been boiling for a week."

The man brought a battered cup, passed that and the makings through the bars, waiting until Steele rolled a smoke, then held forward a lighted match.

"You think this is the Palace Hotel and I'm your waiter?"

Steele laughed a little. He had known Jesse when the boy had ridden for the Flying A. "Aren't you? The way you season that coffee with your thumb shows a lot of practice."

The deputy grunted. "You won't be so all fired smart when they put that rope collar on you. How does it feel to know you're going to die a few days from now?"

Steele took a long drag of the cigarette, then a swallow of the bitter coffee, and smiled. "I'm not dead yet, Jesse."

"You will be. They don't call old Thornbuck the hanging judge for nothing."

The circuit rider had the reputation of hanging more men than old Roy Bean down in Fort Smith, but it was no longer important to Bob Steele. What was important was to make the best of the time he had left. As soon as Dutch Miller had locked him in here, out of the hearing of anyone else, he had told the deputy where to look for Bella Landers and Don Berry, and Dutch had promised that if he found her alive he would get her out of the country. Waiting for Dutch's return with whatever news he would bring was all that interested Steele now.

Jesse was still at the cell door, shaking his head. "I don't get you, Bob. Seems like a man close enough to hear the angels play their harps would spend his time down on his knees trying to make his peace with the boss up there."

Steele swallowed more coffee. "How long is it since you prayed, Jesse?"

The deputy squared his shoulder, affronted. "Just this morning, mister. You don't know it but I got saved when the Reverend Boyster came through here in June. Dunked me in the river himself and then prayed for my soul all night long."

Steele handed back the empty cup but kept the makings. "Then you're all ready to go any time, aren't you?"

"Jesus no, you idiot. You sure talk crazy."

The deputy took himself off and Steele prowled the little cage, his mind following Dutch Miller. He spent a tense night wondering what Miller would find, when he would return, what news he would bring.

He was waked in the morning by the noise of sawing and hammering outside, and went to the window. Men were working in the courthouse square, which he could see by pressing his face against the bars, looking along the side of the building. Sheriff Hayman was not going to have a prisoner of his executed on any but a proper gallows, and he was making political hay, not waiting for the trial and sentencing, having the thing built now, as though to ballyhoo a coming popular event.

The week had passed without a sign of Dutch Miller. He

did not know what the long absence meant. Dutch should have been back in two days at the most. Or perhaps Dutch had returned and was avoiding him, did not want to tell him what he had found.

Steele had not been without visitors. Every day old Jake was there wheedling, offering to frame somebody to take Steele's place if Steele would tell him where Bella was. Steele had simply turned his back, neither looked at or spoken to Clayborne.

Now, today, the trial that had been delayed a year would open. Steele ate his breakfast with slow, deliberate concentration. He was not afraid but he was tense enough that he did not want the complication of an upset stomach. He was barely finished when two deputies came for him, walked him down the hall and up the steps to the second floor courtroom.

The room was filled with the curious, even the deep windowsills crowded with men sitting like crows on a fence. He looked around him as he walked toward the counsel table where his lawyer waited, thinking that the whole population of Central Park had come in for the show. Court day was always a magnet. Next to the revival meetings put on by itinerant evangelists, watching the functioning of the law was the most exciting entertainment available. The smells of sweat and old dust were strong and flies swarmed, buzzing above the heads.

His lawyer, a man named Diggs, stood up as he reached the table. Steele did not know him, had met him only once when he had been brought to the cell. He was fresh from the East, had been in Walton only three months, a middle-aged man with the stamp of earlier failure about his drooping shoulders. Steele had no money for an attorney and the court had appointed this one. Steele had not protested, knowing that the trial would be a sham no matter who represented him.

Diggs had shown his distress at their first and only interview.

"There is no basis for a defense," Steele had said. "I did not kill Ralph Hume. When we took Berry's cattle home I rode ahead to watch for Hume's crew, and when I hit Berry's boundary I spent the night in the brush where I could spot a raid in time to warn my men. But no one saw me, so I can't prove it."

Diggs had wagged a schoolteacherish finger at him and said solemnly, "The burden of proof is on the prosecution, Mr. Steele."

"Not here, not now. Counselor, you'd better learn about this country or you'll have slim pickings. The prosecution doesn't need to prove anything because the jurors have already decided the verdict."

The lawyer had swelled and huffed. "But I'll challenge them."

"How many challenges do you have, Counselor?"

"Why, I . . ."

Steele pitied the man, a greenhorn who should have stayed in Indiana, and who needed to be told some facts if he were to survive here at all.

"Mr. Diggs," Steele said bluntly, "the only reason the judge appointed you to defend me was that no local lawyer would take my case. They knew better. I was a maverick, worked for a small outfit. The big ranchers won't let their authority be challenged. They own the courthouse and the sheriff's office and they mean to keep control. I had the gall to challenge the biggest rancher in the Park and I took our cows away from him. As long as I am around as an example I'm a threat. Someone else might try to stand against them."

"But . . . but . . . I have to make some kind of defense."

"Put me on the stand, let me tell my story. No one will believe me but you will have gone through the motions."

"I would be derelict. That's no defense at all."

"Then what would you suggest?"

Diggs had sputtered and fussed, but he had no magic surprise, and they sat side by side facing the bench now, saying nothing, waiting while the clerk intoned:

"Hear ye, hear ye, the circuit court for the Territory of Colorado is now in session the Honorable Horace Thornbuck presiding. Please stand."

The room came to its feet, the door behind the bench opened and the judge came through it, a small man, walking like many small men, with a pouter pigeon strut. He did not wear robes. No justice in that territory at that time dared. He wore the knee-length frock coat affected by most gentlemen and all gamblers, a roll-brim bell-shaped derby and a ruffled shirt that rumor said he sent as far as Kansas City to have laundered. Before he took his chair a flurry of movement across the room caught his attention; he reached for his gavel and used it to command silence.

Bob Steele turned to see what the commotion was. The spectators' door had opened and the deputy on guard was clearing a passage. The banker, Albert Thorne, filled the opening with his short, thick figure, followed by his daughter and then Reggie Hume.

Bob Steele had not seen the girl since the morning she had thrown his small diamond at his face through the cell bars, tall, cool-looking blonde with thick, shining braids in a hal around her head. In spite of himself Steele's throat contracted at sight of her.

For all the austerity she had presented to the world there had been a mischief in her that had appealed to him. They had ridden the Park together, gone to the dances at the scattered schoolhouses, and dreamed dreams. Her father had not approved of him, a working foreman with a monthly wage of sixty dollars. He was not the prospective husband Thorne wanted for his only daughter.

But he had been young and Linda had been young, and the physical attraction between them had been very strong. It had been a brutal shock that she could believe he had murdered anyone. He had looked to her as the one person who would believe him without proof being needed.

Now here she was, come to see him convicted. What had drawn her into this exposure that would surely breed gossip? Was she here to gloat because the tarnish on his name had rubbed off on her? Was this her revenge? Or had she come for one last look at the man she had once claimed to love?

As if she felt the pull of his eyes she turned her head and for a long moment their gaze held across the watching room. Then she turned away, but even at the distance he saw the flush that colored her neck and cheeks, and smiled to himself. She might not have faith in him but he still moved her.

His lawyer tugged on his arm, pulling him down to the chair and he became aware that he was the last one standing. Thornbuck opened the court and the attorneys rose to choose a jury. Steele had gone to school with the prosecutor. He would be tried by old acquaintances, none of whom had been close friends, because in so thin a society it was impossible to find twelve men who had not known him. Diggs used up his challenges immediately, and to his question as to whether a man was prejudiced he got a consistent, "Yep," as answer. The prosecutor challenged no one.

With the jury seated he called his witnesses. They marched them through in a day and a half. Claud Hammer, the RH foreman, was last to take the stand. Steele would not have been surprised if Hammer claimed to have seen the murder, but the man contented himself with a description of the argument between Ralph Hume and Steele when Steele had come for Berry's cattle.

With the direct testimony finished Diggs rose to examine Hammer. He had not bothered with the others, whose testimony was at best circumstantial or hearsay, but he made Claud Hammer explain each step in the events of the fateful day.

"You tell us Mr. Hume, Senior, ordered you to round up the Berry cattle and hold them in the ranch corral?"

"That's what I said." Claud Hammer had been born with a chip on his shoulder and he resented this Eastern dude who dared contest against the power of the Hume ranch.

The defense lawyer's eyebrows were raised. "Isn't it a serious crime in this country for one rancher to rustle his neighbor's animals?"

Claud Hammer sneered. "We didn't rustle them. We warned Berry's crew plenty times to keep their critters off our grass."

Diggs affected deep surprise. "Your grass? I understand that most of Central Park is government land, open to all."

"That don't mean nothing. The Humes been running stock near twenty-five years."

"And that gives them squatter's rights?"

Hammer spat tobacco juice at the cuspidor. "A man's got a right to protect his grass."

"By stealing another man's stock?"

"You heard me before. We didn't steal them. We just penned them."

"What were you going to do with them?" Diggs's voice was heavy with sarcasm. "Run the Hume brand on them?"

Hammer threw a badgered look toward the spectators as if in appeal to Reggie Hume to get him out of the witness chair. Diggs snapped at him.

"Answer me."

The foreman wiped a sleeve across his damp forehead. "I don't know . . . Mr. Hume didn't tell me . . . he . . ."

Diggs waited until the voice trailed off, then bore in again. "So he might have been planning to ship them, to kill them, or maybe to return them to Berry if he learned his lesson?"

"Yeah. That's right." Hammer grabbed at the suggestion. "I guess that's what he aimed to do, just teach that little ranch to stay off our graze."

"But Bob Steele had the courage to ride in and take back his boss's property. I assume Ralph Hume was not pleased at that."

"Damn right he wasn't. Steele had us under the gun because we only had four riders at home when he come."

"What did Ralph Hume say at the time? What were his words."

Claud Hammer's face held a dark anger. "I ain't supposed to use them here. He cussed Steele out to a fare-you-well. Said if he ever caught Steele or any of his crew on our place again he'd hang them on the nearest tree."

Diggs turned away, walked down the jury box looking into the eyes of each man in turn, then came back to Hammer.

"Thank you. That is all. You may step down."

Claud Hammer did not understand. He stammered, "But . . . but . . ."

Judge Thornbuck, his chin resting on his fist, said sharply, "Step down."

Claud Hammer left the chair watching Diggs suspiciously. The prosecution rested. Diggs called only one witness, Bob Steele himself, and led him through his story, of taking his crew to the RH, confronting Ralph Hume, taking the animals out of the corral and starting them toward home.

"You rode ahead to see that the trail was clear?"

"That's right."

"You did not circle back to the Hume ranch?"

"I did not. I waited where the trail crossed onto Berry's land to see if Hume would bring his crew."

"Then you could not be the man who killed Ralph Hume?"

"I could not have."

Diggs walked back to his table, passing the prosecutor, saying, "That's all. Your witness."

"No questions. Step down."

Steele sat alone at the counsel table listening to the closing arguments with a detachment as if they did not pertain to him at all. He studied the jurors' frozen expressions, heard Thornbuck deliver his charge, saw the jury trail out, and found nothing to surprise him when ten minutes later they filed back with the announcement:

"Guilty as charged."

Diggs gave vent to a gasp. "This is the baldest miscarriage of justice I ever saw. They had no hard evidence at all."

Steele said: "Their minds were made up a year ago. They can't admit even to themselves that they could possibly be wrong. Thanks for trying anyway."

Chapter 17

The hotels were full. There was a gala campground outside of town where the ranchers from the distant spreads had parked their wagons and tents to be on hand for the trial and where they now lay over to witness the hanging scheduled for the next morning.

The scaffold was finished. Steele watched and listened while the sheriff's deputy tested the trap door with various weights tied to the end of the rope, intent on an exact balance. When the latch was sprung the body must fall with force enough to break the neck. Bob Steele had deliberately blocked out his imagination and still retained the eerie detachment, gift of the girl who had dared to escape Jake Clayborne.

Sheriff Hayman had set the execution with a political eye for ten o'clock, giving time for folks to have their breakfasts and redd up their camps, prepare for the long drives home when the man in the cell was dead and the post-mortem talk was done.

When the slam and thud of the trap door stopped at dusk Steele left the window and sat down on the thinly mattressed strap iron bunk. His last night on earth. Well, there was nothing more he could do about it. He had played out the string. He had not cried nor crawled. Everyone must die sooner or later and at least this way was quick and said to be painless.

Noise in the corridor drew his attention and he was not surprised when Reggie Hume stopped outside his bars. He nodded without standing up, knowing that Hume had come to gloat, enjoy the satisfaction of Steele breaking and begging. Bob Steele disappointed him with an easy grin.

"You primed for the big show, Reggie?"

Hume snarled. "I'm going to enjoy it a lot longer than you are."

Steele tilted his head. "At least you can watch it through."

Hume started another baiting, stopped it, changed his tactic and said almost querulously, "Now that it's all over and there's no chance you won't hang why don't you ease your conscience? Admit you did kill my father."

"I wouldn't want a lie on my lips now." He rose then and walked casually to the bars. "You got an extra cigarette?"

Without thinking that he gave something his enemy wanted Hume pulled a sack and papers from his shirt pocket and passed them through. Steele rolled his smoke, smiling faintly, returned the makings and when Hume had made himself a cigarette and struck a sulphur match, held his through the bars. Hume lit it absently.

Steele said, "Reggie, you're letting something very different from murder blind you. It could be dangerous for you."

The man's eyes brooded on him. "What's that mean?"

Steele filled his lungs with smoke and let it out as he spoke. "You and Linda in court together this morning. You want me dead because of her."

"Shut up." There was sudden, vicious rage in the voice.

"The rope will shut me up tomorrow. Until then I'll talk. You may marry her, but you won't be rid of me. You'll never know how she rates you against me. And I know I'm the better man."

Steele smiled openly as Hume's fists clenched convulsively. It was a real pleasure to bait the baiter.

"But there's more for you to worry about. If I did not kill your father, who did? He can be walking up and down that street now, laughing at you. He may even be a threat to you."

Hume's eyes went through Steele, looking at an idea he had never thought of, so close had his concentration been on clearing Steele out of his path to Linda Thorne, and his face was open, blank with fear. Then he spun away and charged out through the office. Steele heard him slam the outer door behind him. A minute later Hayman came down the corridor.

"What did you say to Reggie? He went out like he had a firecracker go off under his tail."

Steele gave him a genuine smile. "I gave him an idea. It hurt. I asked him, if I didn't kill his father, who did."

Hayman's eyes narrowed, then he returned the smile. He had spent his professional life licking Ralph Hume's boots and then catering to Reggie and he had no love for either.

"That ought to give him something to chew on whether it's true or not. Guess I'll put a guard outside here. From the way he looked I wouldn't put it past him to come to the window and shoot you tonight."

"And that would be a shame, Sam, after all the work of building that scaffold and you counting on everybody coming to see your show. Give them what they want and they'll re-elect you. They'll stand gawking like they do at a freak show until they've seen my neck stretched, then they'll unpack their lunch baskets and sit down on the courthouse grass and eat and watch me swing back and forth, back and forth."

The sheriff had quit smiling. His heavy face paled, took on a greenish tinge. "God, Bob . . . You must be loco. Murder trial . . . death sentence is enough to make anyone crack up . . . God . . ."

He hurried off along the corridor. Steele sat down on the bunk again. The echo of his words did not sound nearly so amusing as he had meant to make them.

Time was passing too quickly, or not quickly enough. Steele wished he had something to do, work, a deck of cards, anything to occupy himself. Even a cigarette. But he thought Hayman would not come near his cell again. He would have to wait until the deputy brought his supper. He lay down and forced himself into a half sleep.

Supper surprised him. The jail food had been poor, cooled on its trip from the Chinaman's down the block, but tonight the tray was crowded with heavy crockery that held the heat, brought from the nearest hotel dining room. He lifted the napkin covering and looked at a big steak, mashed potatoes, beans, and sourdough biscuits. He picked up the tray the deputy had shoved under the bottom bar of the door.

"Somebody have a change of heart?"

The man grunted. "Sam didn't think a man ought to be sent to hell on an empty gut. Me, I don't see what difference it makes whether you burn full or burn hungry."

"Thanks."

Steele set the tray on the three-legged stool that served as his table. He ate slowly, relishing each bite. By now he should have recovered from the hunger of his long chase but he still felt as if he had not eaten for a year. When the dishes were mopped clean he poured a second cup of coffee. The deputy had brought the whole pot that was kept on the office stove. Then he called the deputy, surrendered the tray, asked for tobacco and rolled his smoke.

It was luxury not to be running, to sit here quietly, sipping the hot coffee unhurriedly, smoking in leisure.

The cell darkened as night fell. It came to him that this was the last dark he would see before it became permanent, and for a moment his new courage faltered. He set his jaw tightly. The last thing he wanted was that Reggie Hume, anyone, would see him show fear.

When the cigarette burned his lips he threw the butt in a corner and lay down without undressing. Sounds from the town filtered to him. The click of hoofs on hard ground. The murmur of men's voices. An occasional laugh. A shrill scream that came through the night from Miss Mary's, whose house abutted the rear of the courthouse. Going between the house and the saloons the girls took pleasure in peering through the jail windows, making lewd comments to the caged men.

Steele would have welcomed even that to break the monotony of waiting. He tried to sleep and could not. The night slipped on and the street noises lessened, then faded, leaving only the light tinkle of pianos behind closed saloon doors.

Steele strained to hear any sound, to guess at its origin, a game to fill the minutes. Suddenly there were horses in front of the courthouse, a racket of angry shouts there. The outer door of the jail office slammed open. A familiar voice bellowed curses as a man was dragged, fighting, along the corridor.

Steele was off the bunk, standing at the grille when the

new prisoner was hauled past and flung into the last cell in the row. It was old Jake Clayborne, being manhandled by two strangers who were certainly no deputies of Sam Hayman. Jake was like a mad bull, yelling, shaking the bars, stamping up and down the cell, cursing with every step. Steele watched him through the bars of the cell that separated them, and called:

"What's happened?"

"That damn woman." The roar bounced off the corridor walls. "I wish I'd never bought her. Never heard of her. I wish Red Cloud had cut her throat. She's purely trouble."

Steele caught the bars so tightly they cut into his hands. "You mean she's all right?"

"Right as rain and mean as a cornered snake. She went to the capital and swore out a warrant for me . . . kidnapping . . . slavery . . . I don't know what all. She rode in here with a pair of federal marshals that routed me out of bed in the hotel and clapped me in this bird cage."

Steele whooped as loud as Jake. "Hooray for Bella. She did it. She did it."

Jake shook a big fist toward him. "It's your fault. If I hadn't laid over to watch you swing I'd be safe up in the hills. There ain't a federal marshal alive that can take a Clayborne out of the Medicines."

Sheriff Hayman came down the corridor and stopped at Steele's door, used a big key to unlock the grille and swing it wide.

"Come on, boy."

Steele had a bad moment thinking that for some reason his execution had been moved up. "Come where?"

"Judge wants to see you."

Jake Clayborne yelped. "Hey, what is this?"

174

"None of your business." Sam Hayman had had more than enough of old Jake this last week.

Steele stepped out of the cell, pausing, expecting to be handcuffed. Instead Hayman walked away, holding the office door open for him. There was not even a gun at his belt. An impulse to run shook Steele. If he could make the livery, get a horse . . . But as he stepped past Hayman the sheriff said:

"You're a damn lucky man to have a woman like that."

The impulse to escape died. If Bella was responsible for whatever was going on he could only spoil it by running again. He walked into the open night at Hayman's side and down the empty street to the hotel and into the lobby.

There was a group of men clustered around one corner of the room. Steele could see only their backs until the sound of his entrance with Hayman brought them about and apart.

He did not see her at once. He saw the two federal deputies standing, saw Don Berry's lawyer hunched nervously between them, saw Judge Horace Thornbuck sitting in an upholstered chair too big for him, looking uncomfortable without his desk in front of him. He saw Dutch Miller facing him, smiling. Then he found her, all but hidden behind Miller in a chair beside the judge. He craned and Miller stepped out of the way, and there was Bella Landers, one side of her face bandaged, her gamin grin stretching her mouth.

Judge Thornbuck patted her hand where it lay on the arm of her chair and said in a gruff tone that might have been apology, "You're a free man, Bob Steele."

Steele's mouth fell open and he stared at the judge. "I . . . I . . . ?"

Thornbuck said, "Tell him, girl, it's your right."

Steele looked to her, dazed and she nodded. "The governor pardoned you, Bob."

He reached for support, caught the back of a chair and hung on, seeing the shine of her eyes, holding to that. "But why? What for?"

She glanced up at Dutch Miller, then back. "Because we convinced him you didn't kill Ralph Hume. Don Berry did."

He wet his lips with his tongue. This was too fast to comprehend yet. "Berry. Where is he?"

"In the canyon. Dead. His ribs were broken in the fall and I think one went through his lungs. I couldn't do anything for him. He lived three days."

"But . . . ?"

"He was conscious most of the time and kept begging me not to leave him alone there. I said I'd stay if he told me the truth about Hume's death. Write it down. He wouldn't, until I started to climb the bank, then he called me back and told me to get an envelope and pencil out of his saddlebags that were still on the dead horse . . . I held him while he wrote the confession and signed it. He died that night, but I couldn't get out of the canyon alone.

"Then Mr. Miller showed up on top and threw a rope down to haul me out and took me to the governor. The governor insisted that the writing had to be identified as Berry's. The only one I thought of who could do that was Berry's lawyer friend Billingsly and the governor wanted to send a marshal to bring him to the capital, but Mr. Miller told him how little time there was and I pleaded with him, so he came here with us. Mr. Miller made Billingsly show us some of Berry's letters and the writing matched, then Mr. Miller made

Billingsly admit Berry was not with him the night of the killing, wasn't in town."

Bob Steele had to pull the chair around and sink into it. His knees would not hold him up any longer. He looked from one face to another, hardly believing.

"What did Berry write? How did he happen to go to Hume's place? They hated each other. Did he intend to bushwhack Hume?"

"He claimed not. He said Hume sent for him, left a letter at the post office saying the cattle had been impounded and would be held until Berry agreed to sell the ranch to Hume. It made Berry furious. He said he rode into the RH yard to tell Hume he wouldn't sell no matter what and he'd take the letter to court. He said Hume went for his gun and he shot in self-defense."

"But no gun was found with Hume's body . . ."

"Berry said it was there when he left, that it dropped close beside Hume. He suspected that when Claud Hammer found his boss he took the gun away to make it look like murder."

"But why didn't Berry . . . ?" Steele stopped. He knew the answer even as he asked the question. Berry knew he would have gotten no more justice in a Walton court than Steele had. Berry had kept quiet and tried to salve his conscience by breaking Steele out of jail and giving him a horse.

Now Berry was dead and Steele was free. He would not hang. He pulled in a long, savored breath, held it, and let it out, more conscious of breathing than he had ever been.

"Thank you, Bella. Thank you all. Very much."

Chapter 18

<<<<<<<<<<<<<<<<<<<<<<<<<<<<<<<<<<<<<<<<<<<<<<<<<<<<

Bella Landers retreated to the hotel room the governor had taken for her. She would have liked to stay, but she wanted to talk to Bob Steele alone, not with all the men there looking on, so she would wait until he came to her. He looked so thin, so drawn. She hoped they would not keep him long, but it looked as if the judge wanted to hold the stage and make a ceremony.

The meeting in the lobby went on. The night clerk slipped out with the news of the governor's pardon and the word swept through the town. It reached Reggie Hume where he sat in a quiet poker game at the Palace Saloon. He cashed in his chips and hurried to the hotel, furious, making no effort to hide it, raging to the judge and the room at large.

"What right has the governor to issue a pardon on evidence as flimsy as that? He's politicking as bad as Hayman. Where is he?"

Thornbuck's eyes were cold, his voice cold. "If he were politicking he'd be down here showing himself. He went to bed as soon as he signed the pardon. Go home, Hume, and think about how close you came making all of us murderers."

Hume glared at him, glared at Steele, ground around on his heel and went out, slamming the door hard enough that the glass broke and fell behind him. Judge Thornbuck watched after him, then studied Steele, considering, saying in a mild voice:

"I don't think that man likes you."

"I know."

"I don't often give free advice, but if I were in your shoes I'd move as far away from this country as I could get. Reggie Hume swings a very large loop and I suspect there is more than one man riding for him who'd think nothing of crowding you into a quarrel if he thought it would make points with his boss."

"Thanks again," Steele said. "That's advice I mean to take."

There was nothing to hold him here, no relatives, no friend except Sing Ho. He stood up and said good night. He wanted to climb the stairs, go to Bella, but with all the eyes on him he could not. A man could not go into a woman's hotel room at this hour without damaging her.

He paused on the street to appreciate this night that would not after all be his last. He had no money for a room, had given it all to Lily Murphy for the painted horse, and a stubborn pride kept him from asking a loan of any of the men in the lobby.

He looked both ways along the empty street. The night deputy would let him sleep in the jail but the idea of entering a cell again made him ill. He turned toward the livery. The stables of the West had for years been havens for riders

179

caught in towns with no place to sleep. There was hay for a soft pallet and old horse blankets draped across the sides of the box stalls. He walked into the runway where the night hostler napped in a chair tilted against the office wall.

"Borrow a bunk?"

The man had been an eager spectator at the trial, had looked forward to the hanging and now felt cheated. Without getting up he said:

"Lucky stiff. You must have something on the governor to get that pardon."

"No. He just believed the proof."

The hostler shrugged. "So take the end stall, but don't snore. I want to get a little sleep myself."

Bella Landers sat on the edge of the swayback bed in the dress the governor's wife had given her, in the flurried rush to be on the way back, so big she felt lost in its folds, and waited for Steele.

She was drained of emotion, of energy. The demands put on her through the past weeks had sustained her, but now the pressure was lifted, leaving her empty. She could sleep for a solid week, she thought. But not until she had seen Bob Steele. He had stopped running. Dutch Miller had told her how, after Doc Boardman caught him he had given not another inch, had taken all the punishment he was given in the hills and when they had brought him back to consciousness he had held his head high, gone to face whatever waited him without a whimper or a cringe. She smiled to herself, proud of him.

Yet she was uncertain. The trouble they had been through together had drawn them close. Now that they were both out of the dangers how would he feel toward her? They were really strangers. What basis could there be for any relationship when they met again?

An hour passed. She went to the door, opened it, listened at the head of the stairs. The lobby was silent. The meeting was over. He had not come.

She went back to the bed and sagged onto it, wondering. Perhaps the governor had sent for him to talk to him personally. That would be a good political move, and all politicians made capital of everything they could. He was staying with Sheriff Hayman, had not come to the meeting because he was exhausted by the hard ride from the capital, a race against time, but with an hour or so of rest he could have decided that the moment was important. Then she shook her head. No. She was fabricating, inventing reasons. Steele simply had not come.

A knock on the door brought her up quickly, running to open it, almost singing her words before she knew who was outside.

"Come in, come in, come in."

It could not be anyone but Bob at this time of night. Then she froze. It was not Steele facing her in the open doorway. It was a woman she had never seen before.

The woman said without smiling, "I am Linda Thorne," in a tone that told Bella she was supposed to recognize the name.

"I don't understand." Bella stood frozen.

Linda Thorne was coming in. Bella had to step aside, out of the way. The visitor shut the door.

"You don't know who I am?"

The name was familiar, but in her disappointment Bella did not know why. She shook her head without speaking.

"I was Bob's fiancée," Linda Thorne said.

The shock of it made Bella blurt, "The girl who threw his ring at him when he was in jail . . ."

Linda's pretty mouth turned down sorrowfully. "A terrible mistake. I'll never forgive myself. I knew it when I did it, but . . . but . . . well, it doesn't matter now. I came to thank you for doing all you did, for giving Bob back to me alive."

"Giving him . . . ?" The words died to a faint gasp.

So this was why Steele had not come tonight. He had run back to this smooth, round, blond face. And not had the courage to come to tell her himself . . . Linda was going on.

"After all, the story is all over town. Jesse White heard that horrible Medicine County sheriff raving about you living with the Indian and then with him when he bought you. I feel sorry for you, but Bob wouldn't want . . ."

"Get out of here."

The girl didn't move. "And think of Bob . . . he hasn't any money, not even a job. What could you do for him but be a burden?"

Through stiff lips Bella asked, "What can you do?"

Linda Thorne's eyes went round and wide. "Why . . . my father owns the bank. He could give Bob a job there, or buy him a ranch. The Berry place will be for sale now."

Bella lifted her head. "Bob Steele would never take that kind of help from a woman."

"Of course he would. He'd be a fool not to. I can't live on a cowboy's pay."

"I think you had better leave now."

Linda looked her up and down in a deliberate comparison between them, then with a tight triumphant smile walked

182

out. Bella stood rigid, staring at nothing, then slowly went toward the wall and looked into the crazed mirror. The bandaged face she saw there was gaunt, hollow, her yellow colored hair falling lank around it. As against Linda's plump, pink throat her neck was a skinny spindle.

"Of course he couldn't love you." She said it aloud to her image. "Who could . . . and after the things that happened?"

In a wrench of decision she flung around, went through the door and tiptoed to the head of the stairs. The other girl was gone, the lobby silent, dim, the lamp turned low on the clerk's desk. She slipped down the steps, passed the man dozing on the stool, opened the outer door softly and went out.

The horse she had ridden from the capital was at the livery. She crossed the gallery, stepped down to the sidewalk and turned toward the barn. Her broken boots made a hollow sound on the boards, but there was no one to hear. Walton was asleep.

The hostler slept on the cot in the office. A lantern burned on the runway wall, showing her the horse and the saddle hung on the stall side. She threw a blanket over the animal's back and lifted the heavy saddle up and cinched it. The far stirrup knocked against the stall as she backed the animal out and when she turned it toward the entrance the hostler was standing in her way.

"Hey. What are you doing?"

"Getting my horse."

He squinted against the yellow lantern light. "The marshals said you was going back to the capital with them tomorrow . . ."

She was already in the saddle, beating her heels against

the horse's flank. It started forward in a jump and the hostler had to dodge aside to keep from being run down. He yelled after her as she bolted into the street, swearing loudly.

Bob Steele scrambled off the hay and looked over the top of the stall. "What's the matter?"

The man swung on him, shifting his anger. "It's that damn woman that got you pardoned. Sneaked in and took her horse and damn near run over me."

"Which way did she go?"

"I don't know and I don't care. I hope she breaks her neck."

Steele was out of the stall as if the hay had caught fire. "My horse . . . Where is it?"

"You ain't got no horse." The man sounded maliciously pleased. "Sheriff sold it. Figured you wouldn't need it where you was going."

"Then I'll take his. Which is it?"

"Oh no you don't. The governor's pardon don't entitle you to steal horses."

"He took mine. It's a fair trade. I'm taking it."

"Over my dead body you will."

Steele jumped for the office, for the shotgun hanging above the desk, and swung back with it leveled on the hostler. "Might be a good idea." He cocked the Greening. "Get the horse. Saddle it. Fast."

The man moved, saddled the animal, brought it out, his eyes popping, held the head while Steele flung up, and jumped back, daring only to raise a protesting hand as Steele drove out, taking the gun with him.

The town was so quiet he could hear the drum of hoofs in the distance. He spurred toward the sound but it was two miles before he pulled abreast. The girl had heard a rider behind her, did not know who it was but had no trust and wanted no truck with anyone, and tried to outrun the other animal. She did not look behind, did not recognize the man who came up beside her until he called her name.

"Bella . . . Bella . . . What's the idea? Pull up."

She pulled up but backed her horse away. "What are you doing here?"

"Chasing you."

"Why?"

"Do you need to ask that? Bella, why do you want to ride out of my life?"

"It's better for you that way. She made me understand."

"She?"

"Your girl."

"I've only got one girl." He kicked his horse against hers, caught her rein, wrapped one arm around her and kissed her.

She fought free and sat stiffly. "Not me. She said her father would give you a job, buy you a ranch . . ."

"Forget her. I never want to see her again."

"But . . ."

"But what? You mean you don't want me?"

"You can't want me . . . after Red Cloud . . . after old Jake . . ."

"I can want you. I do. I don't want anyone else. Bella, we'll go to the capital and get married and I'll find a job. But let's move. I want to be long gone before Hayman finds out I took his horse."

"You stole it? Oh, Bob, you've been in enough trouble. The hostler must know who took it. Take it back before Hayman has you arrested."

"I doubt he will."

"Why wouldn't he?"

He caught her again, kissed her, held her until she relaxed and returned the kiss, then laughed at her.

"So you love a horse thief?"

"Yes, I do. But what about Hayman?"

"Don't worry. He'd have a little difficulty in explaining what gave him the right to sell the horse I rode in here. It belonged to one of the Claybornes. Jake borrowed it to bring me out of the hills."

"Oh." Her smile started, widened, broke into laughter. "Then I know we'd better ride. I don't want that clan after me again."

They wheeled the animals down the road at an easy stride, their saddles almost touching. He grinned across at her.

"You don't say? Look who's running now."

"Well . . . I guess there are times . . ."

Todhunter Ballard was born in Cleveland, Ohio. He was graduated with a Bachelor's degree from Wilmington College in Ohio, having majored in mechanical engineering. His early years were spent working as an engineer before he began writing fiction for the magazine market. As W. T. Ballard he was one of the regular contributors to *Black Mask Magazine* along with Dashiell Hammett and Erle Stanley Gardner. Although Ballard published his first Western story in *Cowboy Stories* in 1936, the same year he married Phoebe Dwiggins, it wasn't until *Two-Edged Vengeance* (1951) that he produced his first Western novel. Ballard later claimed that Phoebe, following their marriage, had co-written most of his fiction with him, and perhaps this explains, in part, his memorable female characters. Ballard's Golden Age as a Western author came in the 1950s and extended to the early 1970s. *Incident at Sun Mountain* (1952), *West of Quarantine* (1953), and *High Iron* (1953) are among his finest early historical titles, published by Houghton Mifflin. After numerous traditional Westerns for various publishers, Ballard returned to the historical novel in *Gold in California!* (1965) which earned him a Golden Spur Award from the Western Writers of America. It is a story set during the Gold Rush era of the 'Forty-Niners. However, an even more panoramic view of that same era is to be found in Ballard's *magnum opus, The Californian* (1971), with its contrasts between the *Californios* and the emigrant gold-seekers, and the building of a freight line to compete with Wells Fargo. It was in his historical fiction that Ballard made full use of his background in engineering combined with exhaustive historical research. However, these novels are also character-driven, gripping a reader from first page to last with their inherent drama and the spirit of adventure so true of those times.

Home Library Service (For Staff Use Only)

1	2	3	4	5	6	7	8	9
		326A						